THE RESISTANCE GIRLS REVISITED

A REUNION OF COURAGE AND BOND

A RESISTANCE GIRL NOVEL
BOOK 8

HANNAH BYRON

There are a thousand ways to kneel and kiss the ground; there are a thousand ways to go home again.

— RUMI

Cover designer: EbookLaunch
Editor: Amber Fritz-Hewer
Website: Hannah Byron
ISBN Ebook: 978-90-833027-3-7
ISBN Paperback: 978-90-833027-4-4

PREFACE

Writing the eight books in *The Resistance Girl Series* has been a literary journey spanning four years for me. The idea for the WWI Prequel, *In Picardy's Fields*, came to me during the summer of 2019 when I visited the Somme region in Picardy, France.

I went to Thiepval and surroundings for research and to pay homage to my great-uncle Jack Westcott, who died in the trenches at the age of 21 in 1915.

Initially I envisioned *The Resistance Girl Series* as a trilogy, centered around two couples, Agnès and Alan, alongside Madeleine and Gerald, who are introduced in the WWI prequel.

I planned for their daughters to become friends at the Swiss finishing school Le Manoir before the war and then join the Resistance movements in England and France during the war. Lili in *The Diamond Courier* and Océane in *The Parisian Spy*.

However, during the writing of the third book a new character, Esther, introduced herself to the friends at the finishing school and the fourth book, *The Norwegian Assassin*, was born.

By the time Book 4 came out in 2022, readers around the world told me they loved *The Resistance Girl Series*, so I decided to add the stories of three more resistance girls, all of whom crossed paths with each other during their pre-war finishing school days in Lausanne under the supervision of Madame Paul. Sable in *The Highland Raven*, Edda in *The Crystal Butterfly,* and Anna in *The London Spymaker.*

Why stop after 7 books, you may ask? While the prospect of introducing more characters in this series remains interesting, I've come to the realization that I deeply long to honor real-life resistance heroines by writing their stories.

This is what I will do in my upcoming series, "Timeless Spies", a dual timeline series about the 39 female secret agents of the SOE Section F.

In the afterword, I'll share my own sentiments about the eight women who have left an indelible mark on this series: Agnès, Madeleine, Lili, Océane, Esther, Sable, Edda, and Anna. They hold a special place in my heart. But I won't delay you any longer from immersing yourself in their stories for the final time.

Join "the girls", now mature women three years after the war, as they come together for a reunion at Madame Paul's finishing school, commemorating her 30th anniversary as Le Manoir's headmistress.

Please keep in mind that the finale only makes sense if you've read all the other books in the series. It's the only book in the series that isn't a standalone novel.

Without further ado, I present to you *The Resistance Girls Revisited*!

Wishing you a lovely read,

Hannah Byron

PART I

THE LETTER

JANUARY 1948

1

THE INVITATION

Le Manoir, Lausanne, 1 January 1948

As the first morning light of 1948 shimmered through the ornate windows of her school office, Madame Paul Vierret sat perfectly straight in her office chair with a sense of solemn resolution.

Thirty years. It both felt like an eternity and the blink of an eye since she took on the mantle of headmistress of the posh finishing school on Lake Geneva.

Her gaze drifted to the grand oak desk before her, polished to a reflective shine, bearing the mental and emotional weight of countless decisions made over the decades.

The office itself exuded an air of timeless elegance. Gold-framed paintings adorned the mauve walls, depicting scenes of friendly Swiss landscapes and 19th-century portraits.

A crystal chandelier hung from the ceiling, casting a glow over the room and its owner. The warm yellow light was the only soft touch to an otherwise stern space.

Beyond the tall school windows, the choppy waters of Lake Geneva stretched out, rippling waves shimmering cold and ruthless in the January morning.

Across the lake, the majestic Savoy Alps rose like silent sentinels, their snow-capped peaks piercing the sky. This same dramatic view had greeted Madame Paul each morning for three decades, yet it never failed to stir something deep within her.

Because, stirred she was, more so this morning than any other morning. Everyone was still in their rooms, both the staff and the students. Not that there were many present, as most had gone home for the Christmas holidays and weren't expected to return for two weeks.

Breakfast would be served in half an hour, and by that time, Madame Paul would need to be in full control of herself again.

For, amidst the beauty of her surroundings, there lingered a dark shadow, a secret carefully concealed behind a mask of impeccable manners and steely resolve. A shadowy secret she allowed to surface only when alone in the sanctuary of her closed-door office.

Madame Paul's celestite blue eyes, sharp and unyielding, belied the turmoil that churned beneath the surface. Her always well-coiffed hair with the roll in the nape of her neck, now streaked with strands of silver, spoke of a lifetime spent maintaining an unassailable facade.

The tailored, navy silk dress hugged her slim figure and the reading glasses on the pearl strings never sported a speck of dust.

For all her years at Le Manoir, Madame Paul knew she'd been a mystery to her students, an authoritarian figure shrouded in enigma.

Whispers of her strict demeanor, her unyielding discipline, and her occasional unfair treatment filled the corridors and the dorms. But none of them fathomed the true depths of her past, the pain that lay hidden beneath that composed exterior.

The Sphinx, she thought. *They call me the Sphinx behind my back. How accurate, how very accurate indeed.*

Lost in thought, Madame Paul's gaze drifted to the polished surface of her desk, where a pristine white paper awaited her attention.

It was time to extend an invitation, to reach out to those who had once passed through the hallowed halls of Le Manoir and left an indistinguishable mark upon its history. Upon her history. And the world's.

With a steady hand, Madame Paul picked up her Parker pen and pulled the sheet of paper towards her. But then, she hesitated. Normally, her words flowed forth with a sense of purpose and efficiency, but nothing came right now. Suddenly plagued by one image, one image only, she closed her eyes.

A tall, blond girl with sad green eyes staring at her in disbelief. Esther Weiss. The eyes full of tears asked wordlessly why *she* was punished when she'd done nothing wrong?

It was a reflection of herself, the mirror she'd looked into before she became Madame Paul Vierret. When she was still Elsie Goldschmidt. Another light-haired, light-eyed Jewess, living her life in secrecy. A lifetime of regrets.

This was her chance to make amends, to bridge the divide that had long separated her from her former students, to lay bare the secrets that had weighed upon her soul for so many years. And the war, that awful war had ripped open all her scars.

Monsieur Paul Vierret in prison for siding with Hitler's Nazi party, organizing the channeling of stolen Jewish property through Switzerland. And she had done nothing. Nothing!

Madame Paul shivered, pulling her fur stole tighter around quivering shoulders.

"Time to make amends." As she spoke the words out loud, her

own voice sounded unfamiliar to her, hollow and metallic. Madame Paul knew the road ahead would not be easy.

But for the first time in decades, she felt a glimmer of hope stirring within her heart, a flicker of light amidst the darkness that had long consumed her.

And so, as the dawn of a new year bathed the world in tentative golden hues, Madame Paul Vierret sat in her Le Manoir office, the blue gaze fixed fiercely upon the future, filled with a longing for reconciliation and redemption.

Le Manoir, 1 January 1948

Chères Anciennes Élèves et Amies,

It is with great joy that I extend this special invitation to you to celebrate a remarkable milestone - my 30th anniversary as the headmistress of Le Manoir Finishing School in Lausanne, Switzerland.

Over the past three decades, I have dedicated my time and energy to the education, growth, and refinement of hundreds of young women who have walked through the doors of Le Manoir and left fully capable to take up their societal places.

In honor of my long career, we are hosting a special celebration at Le Manoir, where former students and friends will come together with the current students and faculty to reminisce and reconnect about their times under my tutorship.

My steadfast dedication to excellence and ongoing influence on generations of students have nurtured women who courageously assumed their roles as mothers, wives, and societal leaders, excelling in diplomacy and behind-the-scenes empowerment.

Yet, among my most esteemed students, there are those who have demonstrated extraordinary courage as resistance women during the recent wars, subsequently forging remarkable careers in peacetime.

These women have applied my teachings in diplomacy and etiquette in an exceptional manner to serve their nations.

It is my express wish to honor this distinguished group of decorated war heroes as special guests during the reunion at Le Manoir.

The celebration will take place on 18 June at Le Manoir on the borders of Lake Geneva, in the heart of our picturesque Swiss countryside.

Festivities will include a gala dinner, musical performances, and heartfelt speeches celebrating both my legacy and those of my guests of honor.

You are invited to stay for the weekend and rooms will be available for everyone at Le Manoir.

I warmly invite you to join us for this joyful occa-

sion as we express our gratitude and admiration for all forms of unwavering dedication and leadership.

Please mark the date on your calendars and RSVP by 15 March 1948.

Avec mes meilleures salutations,

Madame Paul Vierret
Headmistress, Le Manoir

SHE LAID DOWN HER PEN. Folded her hands in her lap and sat like a statue. Outside in the corridor she heard the two maids talking while they headed to the breakfast room.

Soon it would be time to put her mask in place but, by heavens, she was so tired of pretending. To be perfect, to be flawless, to be ever confident. To not be Jewish.

When all this is over, I'll retire, she thought as she rose from her chair and straightened her skirt. As her high-heeled shoes clicked on the marble floor, she straightened her shoulders, painted a modest smile on her coral lips, and turned the doorknob.

LIFE IS BUT A STAGE!

MACBETH.

2

AGNÈS

~ IN PICARDY'S FIELDS ~

Paris, 24 January 1948

In the heart of Neuilly-sur-Seine, in her suburban mansion adorned with ivy-covered walls and trellised windows, Baroness Agnès de Saint-Aubin-Bell enjoyed a moment of quiet solace. Her afternoon cup of Darjeeling tea, her favorite newspaper *Le Figaro*, and today's letters on a silver tray by her side.

A winter sun, weak and watery, filtered through the bay windows, casting a wan glow over the room's elegant furnishings. Delicate gauze curtains covered part of the tall windows, offering a glimpse into the snow-dusted garden where both the alabaster statues and her husband Alan's tropical plants stood wrapped in snow-topped blankets.

The room inside exuded warmth and sophistication, with plush armchairs arranged around a crackling fireplace. Persian rugs, their geometrical patterns woven in vibrant hues, covered parts of the polished parquet floor, while a Rococo clock with a male and female angel holding the marble clockwork ticked like a steady heartbeat.

On the mahogany coffee table before Agnès, a fine porcelain teapot steamed on its warming plate, the fragrant aroma mingling with the scent of Alan's weekly gift of red roses.

Despite her fifty-one years, Baroness Agnès's hair was as light-blond and curly as it had ever been, and on a casual Saturday such as this one, tied together with a slim Hermès scarf. Her China-blue eyes reflected the fire's flickering light as she sat serenely in one of the armchairs immersed in reading the daily news.

Despite her outward appearance of frailty, there was an undeniable strength in her demeanor, a testament to her decades spent as a renowned surgeon at the WWI frontlines, then in Alan's native Chicago, and now back where it all had started, at the American Hospital in Paris.

As she cradled her teacup in her delicate yet capable hands, Agnès took a moment to look up from reading to savor the tranquillity of the sitting room. The hectic pace of her workweek faded into the background, replaced by a sense of calm and contentment.

Alan had taken the boys, Arthur and Daniel, to the ice-skating rink in Boulogne-Billancourt and Colette, Agnès's help in kitchen and house, had gone to the market to get the groceries for the family's extended Sunday lunch.

In that fleeting moment of respite, Agnès found solace in the simple pleasures of life she'd cherished since childhood: a warm cup of tea, the company of her thoughts, and the enjoyment of some sort of reading material - whether a novel, a magazine or in this case the latest news on Parisian life through the eyes of respected journalists.

Added to this was the anticipation of learning the contents of a letter that had arrived that morning from Le Manoir in Switzerland.

Leaning back against the soft cushions of her chair, Agnès breathed a quiet sigh of gratitude. For a short while relieved from the demands of her profession and the responsibilities of her family, she fully savored the beauty of that winter afternoon in Neuilly-sur-Seine, her birthplace, her sanctuary.

Why am I putting off opening the Swiss letter? she wondered as her eyes rested on the angels holding the ticking clock. Agnès had never been to Le Manoir, contrary to most of her peers. She'd already been enrolled at the Sorbonne training as a physician at the age girls from her standing went abroad to obtain their 'finishing school certificate.'

Agnès couldn't but smile. How vividly she remembered her career discussion with her Papa. As usual her father had been all about etiquette and wanting to do right by his one and only adopted daughter.

"But, my dear, all well-educated girls do their finishing school year in some odd-ball institute in the Swiss Alps. What will people take me for? A Neanderthal who didn't know he should send his only girl to the right place to learn how to deck tables and arrange wildflowers?"

Her father's tongue-in-cheek humor was already degrading the institute Agnès herself had no longing to explore, but as usual he would lay the mock blame with her.

"They'll think you a monster of a father," she'd joked back. "However can you defend to your associates that you raised a woman who knows how to wield a surgeon's scalpel, but has no idea where to place the knife with the correct plate on a tablecloth? Oh father, we're a doomed pair."

The Baron's gold-flecked eyes had twinkled, and he'd thrown his elegant hands dramatically in the air.

"Raising a daughter who is so perfect in every sense is so hard on me. Just make sure, you won't come lamenting to me when your husband finds out you have two left hands when it comes to house-keeping skills."

"Papa," Agnès had interrupted his litany with some seriousness,

"I don't care about housekeeping right now. I can always learn that when it's needed. You know I've changed my mind from reading literature to becoming a doctor. I promise you, this is what I want and with the war going on, I need my degree as soon as possible to be of some real help tending to the wounded soldiers. I don't care about anything else."

"Alright, alright, no Le Manoir for *ma chère fille*."

And thus, the situation had been settled. Agnès had never felt she missed something crucial in her life, nor had Alan commented on her 'housekeeping skills,' though he was much more organizational about running the houses where they had lived than she was.

So why had she sent Océane to Le Manoir?

It's true, she admitted to herself, *I was just like Maxipa, afraid my daughter would not have the necessary life-skills training if she didn't go. But then again, Océane had been at a crossroads in her life wanting to give up being a doctor and becoming an artist instead. She'd wanted that gap year herself. It had been different.*

Not that Océane's experience at Le Manoir had been all roses and sunshine. On the contrary. Agnès had heard the stories about Madame Paul from both her friend Madeleine and from her daughter. Each came back with far from positive memories about the teachings and the schoolmarm herself.

Océane might also have received a letter. I'll ask her over lunch tomorrow, Agnès pondered as she slid the paper knife through the top of the crème-colored envelope.

Her eyes flew over the typed lines.

An invitation to Madame Paul's 30th anniversary? In May. As Agnès wondered why she had been invited as a non-attendee at Le Manoir, she heard the front door open, and the boys' excited voices intermingled with the deep voice of her husband.

Agnès folded the letter and put it back in its lined envelope, her blue eyes expectantly directed to the sitting room door that was flung open.

Daniel, her fourteen-year-old adopted son, pushed his older brother Arthur's wheelchair into the sitting room with a practiced swirl of the wheels. The blue eyes of both boys, so alike though not related by birth, shone with glee, their cheeks red with the winter cold.

"Da... Danny pushed me al... all over the ice, Mom," Arthur giggled, struggling to articulate his words because of his excitement, "my... my wheelchair sli... slipped but we had s.. soo much fun!"

"We did!" Daniel agreed slapping his brother on the shoulder, "Thur is a champ at wheelchair sliding, Maman." Both boys spoke French. Daniel the posh Parisian he'd been brought up with and Arthur with the same thick American accent as his father.

"That's great to hear, boys. Now take off your coats and winter boots. Where's Papa gone?"

"We requested hot chocolate and waffles. He's in the kitchen." As Arthur became less wound up about his recent ice-skating adventure, his words came more smoothly, the brain damage due to his bicycle accident ten years earlier less visible.

"You ordered that, huh?" their mother chuckled. "Gosh, you two are becoming the masters of the house, right?"

Daniel gazed at his adopted mother with perplexed uncertainty in the blue eyes. As always when he had a bout of sudden shyness, he blew the fringe from his forehead by letting a pronounced breath escape from his mouth. "It was my doing, Maman. Let me go and help Papa." And out of the room he rushed.

After almost four years of looking after the orphaned boy who'd seen too much during the war, Agnès was used to Daniel's sudden bursts of uncertainty, but she had no idea what set them off.

The boy's moods usually passed as quickly as they came, and after consulting with Doctor Briancourt, a renowned Parisian psychiatrist specialized in war traumas, the new parents had decided to give these bouts as little attention as possible. Any probing into Daniel's past at this stage only tended to upset him further.

And there was always one person who could put the light on in Daniel again and that was his half-sister, Océane. As she was the one who'd found him and taken care of him during the last year of the war together with Madame Noir, the boy idolised her with the affection of a puppy.

Soon Daniel stomped back into the room carrying a tray of delicious smelling waffles, followed on his heels by Alan with the hot chocolate. Agnès smiled up at her husband, her heart skipping a beat, just as when she first saw him as a college student at age eighteen in the spring of 1914.

Doctor Alan Bell, the anchor of Agnès's world for three decades, her lifelong companion and confidant. Despite the years that had gracefully etched their mark on his features, he remained the epitome of dignity and charm.

Agnès's eyes traced the contours of his form, noting the tall stature she had grown so accustomed to over the years. His once-lively brown curls now bore the distinguished hues of silver, a testament to the passage of time. Yet, it was his steely gray eyes that held her captive, their depths reflecting a lifetime of shared joys and sorrows.

As Alan stepped farther into the room, Agnès couldn't help but marvel at the warmth that radiated from his presence. His movements were fluid and purposeful, a testament to the strength and vitality that still coursed through his veins. In his hands, the tray with cups of steaming hot chocolate, still as adroit and precise as ever.

Every move, every gesture he made was simple yet thoughtful and spoke of his love and devotion to her and their children.

"Darling, are we disturbing your peace and quiet?" He placed the tray on the coffee table, his eyes sparkling with an unmistakable affection as he placed a kiss on her forehead.

"Not at all, I can't wait to hear your ice-skating tales."

"Mom, you simply must come next time," Arthur interrupted his mouth full of sugar-coated waffle.

Alan sat down on her arm of her chair and offered her a steaming cup of cocoa. He put his arm around her and together they sat in the intimacy of their shared space. Agnès felt a profound sense of gratitude wash over her.

For Alan, for her boys, for her life. But mainly for Alan. In him, she'd found not only a partner in life, but a kindred spirit whose love had withstood the test of time.

And as they shared a tender smile looking at their boys devouring waffles and discussing the upcoming game of checkers, Agnès knew that whatever might happen in life, this bond, this family would endure for all the years yet to come.

3

MADELEINE

~ IN PICARDY'S FIELDS ~

Lydden Valley Manor, Kent, England, 26 January 1948

In the light-filled sitting room that exuded the mistress's touch for elegance and sophistication, Countess Madeleine de Dragoncourt-Hamilton sat ensconced in a plush armchair, a steaming cup of coffee in her hand.

The morning light, as cool as the North Sea air, filtered through the linen drapes, casting a soft glow over the modern furniture and ornate rugs that gave the room a spacious character.

At her feet, little Zack, her two-year-old grandson, pushed his cars along the edge of the carpet, his 'broom-broom' prattle filling the air like music.

Used to only daughters, Madeleine delighted in his games and followed his every move with great interest. She wasn't averse to getting on her knees in her expensive Dior skirt and racing the cars around the track alongside him. But not now.

With a firm hand, her many rings glittering in the beam of sunshine that filled the room, Madeleine unfolded a letter that had arrived from Switzerland, a school crest emblazoned at the top.

Le Manoir. Heavens, she hadn't thought of the place on Lake Geneva in years. Not since her daughter, Lili, had arrived back from the posh, Swiss finishing school in 1939, looking as miserable after Madame Paul's drillings as she once had been.

As her light-brown eyes danced over the impersonal typed lines, a burst of laughter escaped her lips, surprising even herself. Zack started giggling as well, not knowing the cause of his grandmother's glee but always in for a good joke.

"What funny, Nana?"

"It is all too amusing, my darling!" she chuckled, her English still larded with a strong French accent, "and a slight bit naughty."

"Naughty?" the boy's eyes sought her gaze in confusion, the feline eyes, so like his grandmother, shone with ready curiosity and mischief. "Naughty funny, Nana?" he asked with a smirk.

"I know, darling, but even grown-ups like a bit of naughty at times. Not 'wicked naughty' but 'funny naughty'. You'll know the difference when you're older."

This seemed indeed above Zack's head, and he returned to his cars creating a collision and cheering, "funny naughty."

Madeleine, however, sank back in her chair, remembering her own shades of naughty. It was good Zack was oblivious to his beloved grandmother's rather unusual past.

Confronted with the letter from that past, and babysitting the little cherub at her feet, Madeleine sincerely wondered whether running away from school in 1918 to travel unchaperoned with her pet monkey Loulou to the frontlines in Picardy, where her head could have been blown off any minute, had been a matter of 'funny naughty' or sheer recklessness.

Gerald, her husband, didn't refer to 'the incident' ever again, but Madeleine had sensed from the moment of her arrival at her fami-

ly's war-battered Château near Roye that the young English major
would have protected her with his own life should it have been
necessary. And yet she'd escaped him too, sleek as an eel and prone
to show her worth.

"Nana mad."

Waking from her reminiscence, Madeleine found Zack had
abandoned his cars and nestled himself against her leg. He was
staring up at her with candid concern. She reached down to pick
him up and settled the toddler in her lap.

"Oh no, darling, not mad just thinking," she chuckled kissing the
top of his dark crow., "But thinking this hard will give me wrinkles.
Bah."

"Bah!" Zack mimicked and scrunched up his face.

Madeleine laughed, "wait till you have actual wrinkles of your
own and see if you don't think 'bah!' for real."

Zack again tried to copy her expression. "Bah!"

"Bah, indeed," Madeleine sighed. She certainly didn't like her
wrinkles and had the gray hairs in her thick, auburn hair covered
every six weeks at Minnie's Salon in Deal.

Oh, how wonderful it had been, to be seventeen and full of drive
and passion. She'd give her right hand to be Mad-Maddy all over
again. Suddenly, she missed Loulou with a sharp pang of grief.

In 1919, engaged to Gerald and planning to settle in England,
Madeleine had agreed to hand her pet monkey over to the Zoo of
the Jardin des Plantes in Paris. Loulou had fallen seriously ill and
the little black Spider monkey needed the care of professionals. But
it had been incredibly hard to say goodbye to her beloved
companion.

Whenever in Paris, she'd visited Loulou and spent a couple of
hours with her until the monkey's death, at an unknown age, in 1932.

Madeleine's mind raced with memories of her rebellious youth
and, with her grandson sucking his thumb and resting against her

bosom, she reached for the black telephone on the nearby table and dialed the operator to connect her with Paris.

As she waited for the connection, she glanced down at Zack, his cherubic face with the dark lashes already closed over his eyes. It was time for his afternoon nap, but the phone was already ringing. Another impulsive, ill-timed decision. *Tanpis!*

With anticipation but also some trepidation, Madeleine awaited the connection to her dear friend Agnès, unsure what the reaction would be when told her Madeleine might return to the place she'd always said she hated.

But she was eager to share this odd twist of fate with someone who understood her in ways no one else did, even if Agnès hadn't been to Le Manoir, she knew Madeleine.

"*Bonjour, avec La Bell Residence.*" An unfamiliar French voice, probably the housekeeper, answered the phone. Madeleine suddenly remembered it was Monday. Agnès would be at the hospital.

"Bonjour, Madame. This is Madame Hamilton from England. Please tell Madame Bell I phoned and that I'll call back another time."

"Ah, Madame Hamilton, would you perhaps care to have a word with Madame Riveau? She just dropped by on her way home."

"Océane? Sure, I'd love to."

"Let me get her for you. *Un moment, s'il vous plaît.*"

Océane, now married to her French resistance hero, the painter Jean-Jacques Riveau, was as good a friend to Madeleine's daughter Lili, as Agnès was to her. The four of them met up regularly, either in Paris or on the Kent coast.

"Tante Madeleine?" Océane's sweet voice with its faint American accent sounded in her ear.

"Ah chérie, I totally forgot your mother wouldn't be home on a

Monday afternoon, but never mind. It's lovely to hear your voice instead. Everything well?"

"Yes Tante, would you want me to leave a message for Mom?" Océane still addressed her parents with Mom and Dad. From all the years the family had lived in Chicago, they still upheld many of their American manners.

"No, no need. I'll try again soon. I just wanted to tell her I received an invitation from Switzerland, you know from that finishing school you and Lili and I attended. I'm on the horns of a dilemma. Your mother, wise as always, steered clear of that finishing year in the Alps and hasn't become a lesser society lady for it."

"The letter from Madame Paul?" Océane inquired. "Oh yes, I also got the invitation, and I was going to phone Lili about it tonight. I was just passing by Mom and Dad's place on my way home because I had forgotten the letter over luncheon yesterday. That's when Mom and I discussed it. Do you know what the strange thing is, Tante Madeleine?"

"No, tell me."

Zack stirred in his sleep and Madeleine reduced her voice to a whisper. Océane continued, "Mom got the letter as well. She's invited too though she never attended the school."

"She did? That's odd, or perhaps it has something to do with Madame Paul's words that she wants to give special attention to you and the other girls who are decorated war heroes. Maybe she has invited Agnès and me just as the mothers of the special guests. Did Agnès say she'd be going?"

"But you and Mom also got medals for your work in WWI," Océane protested. "Anyway, to answer your question, Mom was hesitant about the whole affair, but I'm sure she'll tug along if we all decide to go. Have you asked if Tante Elle also got the letter?"

Madeleine thought of her older sister in New York.

"I haven't even had time to ring her. I rang your mother first. But

Elle was at Le Manoir before Madame Paul became headmistress. I was with the first batch that had the pleasure of experiencing the full brunt of her regime."

Océane chuckled, "that sure rings a bell, but didn't you run away, Tante? I remember Lili telling me something of that nature. I also remember Madame Paul rubbing what she called your 'improper behavior' in poor Lili's face whenever she could."

"I know. Mea culpa, mea culpa," Madeleine chortled. "That escapade of running away would be my main reason not to attend this upcoming gathering. I can tell you, Oncle Gerald had to dig deep into his pockets to get Lili into that school on short notice after she turned down Iain's first proposal."

"Gosh, and I thought I was the worst criminal of the pack, having cheated on a medical exam and been expelled from Radcliffe," Océane added.

"Those were our youthful days of defiance and disruption," Madeleine observed, "but we all turned out alright, didn't we? Though Madame Paul may still disagree on that point. Well, ma chérie, give my love to the Bells and the Riveaus and we'll discuss Le Manoir in more detail soon."

"Bye, Tante Madeleine, I'll tell Mom you called. Give Lili a kiss from me and tell her I'll be in touch."

After she put down the receiver, Madeleine sat lost in thought. She couldn't help but wonder about the journey that lay ahead.

This spring Rosalie, the youngest, and surprise, addition to the Hamilton entourage , would turn eight and start her term at Howell's Girls' Boarding School in Denbigh, just like Lili had done twenty years earlier.

Now eighteen, their adopted daughter, Sarah Goldmunz-Hamilton, had started at the Royal Academy of Music to train as a concert pianist. She had settled in the family's flat in Kensington, which Gerald also used when in London for Westminster politics.

After Easter, the Bahamas beckoned with promises of sunshine and relaxation, a welcome escape together with Gerald from the chilly and wet English weather.

But the unexpected invitation to her former school's celebration tugged at Madeleine's heartstrings, stirring memories she had long buried.

Would Madame Paul, the iron-fisted headmistress, still hold Madeleine's teenage indiscretions against her? Or had time softened the edges of their shared history, allowing for forgiveness and reconciliation?

"Let me get you to your cot, sweet one," she whispered in her grandson's tousled hair, as she rose from the chair, stiff from sitting too long. "And then I'll ask Molly to put on the kettle. Lili will soon come in for a cuppa when her work at the Colliery is done."

For some reason, Madeleine could not wait any longer to discuss the surprise letter with her eldest daughter.

4

LILI
~ THE DIAMOND COURIER ~

Later that afternoon

As the icy, North Sea wind whipped across the flat landscape on top of the cliffs near Betteshanger Colliery, Lili Hamilton Brodie made her way towards her parents' home, her slender figure wrapped tightly in a wool coat against the biting cold.

Her short red hair was ruffled by the gusts, and her blue eyes squinted against the red glare of the setting winter sun.

A menacing storm was making rapid progress across the Channel. Thunderous black clouds, striped with white hailstones and snow, hung like heavy drapes over the choppy sea.

Far below her, whipped-up whitecaps topped the wild waves before they crashed on the pebbled beach and clashed against the chalk rocks.

As always, Lili was mesmerized by the force of the elements atop the cliffs, the place of her temperament, her home. The sight of a storm approaching from Cap Gris-Nez on the French coast was always a magnificent spectacle over the open landscape.

Lili felt the elements in every fiber of her being, but this time she didn't wait for the storm to pummel her until she almost toppled over, but hastened indoors before the heavens opened.

She couldn't arrive drenched like a wet cat to pick up her son. Mothers were meant to responsible beings. Well, at least, she tried to be.

Passing quickly by the rows of miners' cottages, she exchanged nods and brief greetings with the hardworking men and women who called the colliery home.

Despite the chill in the air, there was a sense of warmth and camaraderie among them, forged through years of toil and struggle. Lili knew they liked her as their boss, and she liked them in return. Each and every one of them.

Lili's mind drifted as she walked, reflecting on the day working at the colliery. After the war, she'd taken over the management from her father, Sir Gerald Hamilton, with a determination to improve conditions for the miners and their families.

Her socialist ideals drove her to fight for fair wages and better living standards, even in the face of opposition from more conservative quarters.

It made her popular with the workers, but less so with the Westminster politicians who insisted that in an economy needing to recover from the war, everyone had to make sacrifices.

Yet Lili was, and always would be, a fighter for righteous causes, and she wouldn't back down for anyone. Her weekly column in *The Daily Worker* besieged any opponent of her lofty plans to improve life for the British working class.

Her thoughts also wandered to her husband, Iain, and their son Zack. Iain had returned from the war a wounded hero. Instead of returning to his former position as his father-in-law's accountant, he'd chosen a quieter life, pursuing his passion for organic farming.

It was a decision Lili respected and supported wholeheartedly, knowing that true heroism lay not in grand gestures, but in the everyday sacrifices of ordinary people. And she could see how happy he was making sure his family could live off the land.

Arriving at Lynden Valley Manor, Lili's spirits lifted at the thought of tea with her mother, Madeleine, and the prospect of spending some downtime with her young son. 'Maman,' as Lili invariably called her French mother, had been her staunchest supporter after they'd solved their rifts during Lili's teenage years.

Now Maman was her best friend, the one who always encouraged her to pursue her dreams and never back down in the face of adversity. Though her father loved her and respected the way she led his coal mine, he was not in favor of her socialist ideas, which he called 'pushy and unrealistic'.

As always before entering the house, Lili made a detour to the stables, where her mahogany-colored Arabian, her loyal horse of fifteen years, would scrape his hooves and snort loudly as a greeting to his mistress.

"Hello Morning Star, how are you today?" Lili scratched the white fleck on his velvet nose, while feeding him one of Iain's organic carrots. The warmth of his breath was welcome on her chilly hands. "Alas, my dear friend, not a day for a ride. Snow's in the air and it's getting dark already. I'll try to slip out of the office earlier tomorrow afternoon."

Morning Star pushed his soft nose in her neck and Lili suddenly shuddered. An unexpected wave of memories crashed down on her like a relentless tide. It was as if the very air around her shifted, transporting her back to a time of unspeakable horror and despair.

She was still vaguely aware of her horse's presence, usually a source of solace and reassurance, now mingled with the chilling sense of cold, metal bars in a concentration camp - Fort Breendonk in Belgium.

Lili braced herself, this had happened to her before. Despite knowing what was happening, her senses overwhelmed her, and she was sucked back, against her will, to the haunting past she wanted so desperately to bury.

The stench of decay assaulted her nostrils, the acrid smell of human suffering blending with the scent of dirty straw mattresses and stale coal soup. She could almost taste the bitterness of fear and desperation that was choking her, a taste so strong it was poisoning her very soul.

Her ears echoed with the distant cries of anguish, the haunting wails of those who had lost all hope, of those who were tortured, of those who were dragged before the firing squad.

The symphony of recalled suffering was so piercing it almost drowned out the real sounds of Morning Star's gentle whinnies as a reaction to his mistress's anguish. Still, she clung to her horse, to his mere whispers in the storm of memories assaulting her senses.

Lili's skin prickled with the memory of icy cold - the biting chill of despair that had seeped into her bones during those endless nights in the camp. She could feel the weight of exhaustion pressing down on her, each step a struggle against the overwhelming urge to surrender to oblivion.

But amidst the darkness, there was a flicker of light. A warmth that emanated from Morning Star, a beacon of comfort in the midst of the raging storm. He knew the extent of her distress; he knew like no other. The Arabian nuzzled even closer against Lili's shivering body, stopped his whinnying, now offering silent companionship and unwavering support.

There, there now. Be calm. Be still. You are safe now. You are safe with me.

And in that moment, Lili found herself clinging to that lifeline, drawing strength from the bond they shared. For, even in the depths of her darkest memories, there was a glimmer of hope. A reminder that no matter how harrowing the past, there was always a way forward, guided by the steady rhythm of hoofbeats and the unwavering light of morning.

As the flashback began to fade, leaving Lili shaken but resilient, she buried her face in Morning Star's mane, breathing in the familiar scent of trust and understanding. Together, they stood as a testament to the unbreakable bond between horse and rider.

"I need to find help," she sobbed against Morning's Star's neck. "Iain is right, I need to find help. I am not okay."

It took Lili another ten minutes to steady her breath, dry her tears, and feel enough control over her emotions to face her mother and son.

"Thank you, dear horse." She gave Morning Star some extra fresh hay to munch and a last loving pat. "I don't know what I should do without you. Never, ever leave me, Star."

On shaking legs, Lili entered the house through the back door, while the first hail stones pelted the patio. A welcome warmth from well-stoked hearths greeted her. She was still shivery and shaken.

Calling a muffled 'hello' to Molly, their loyal housekeeper of twenty years, Lili shed her coat and went in search of her mother. As she opened the sitting room door, she was glad to see Maman was alone, as Zack was still down for his afternoon nap.

"*Mais non, chérie,* what has happened to you? You look pale as the waning moon." Her mother rose from the chair where she had been sitting reading a novel, moving with swift steps towards her daughter.

Tall and willowy, with the elegance of the French countess she was, Madeleine wrapped her long arms around her trembling eldest child. Lili let herself be held, grateful for her mother's strength, unable to stop her tears from streaming down her cheeks.

"Oh Maman, those images from the past are killing me. I thought they were gone after Zack was born, but they're back and they're killing me."

"*Ah ma pauvre petite*. Come, come, and sit down and I'll ring for a fresh pot of hot tea. You feel as if you're frozen all over."

"I went to the stables on my way here," Lili explained through rattling teeth while Madeleine rang the bell with a firm gesture. Then she wrapped Lili in a soft cashmere blanket and held her close.

They sat huddled together on the couch when Molly, who seemed to never need any instructions, strode in with a tray with a tea pot and the afternoon sandwiches.

Even Molly sensed when Lili was in the grip of her past. Though the flashbacks had lessened over the past two years, the whole family knew the extent of the diamond courier's concentration camp memories.

"It's so strange," Lili said with a stronger voice after having sipped the hot tea. "One moment, I feel like I can take on the whole world and then, out of nowhere it seems, I'm tackled by these memories. They are so vivid and so sudden, like flashing lightning. I have no way to predict when they come to haunt me. What am I to do, Maman? I feel embarrassed by myself."

"There's absolutely no reason to feel embarrassed, *ma fille*, but I do think it's time you spoke with our good, old Doctor Finchley. He told me the other week that they're having good results with war trauma treatments in some clinic in London. Talk to him, Lili. We all want you to overcome the horrors that keep haunting you. I will never forget how I found you in that Antwerp field hospital. You were so thin, so weak, so sick. Maybe it's time to face your demons, no matter how hard it will be, and free yourself from them for good."

Lili nodded. With her mother close by and warmed by the

blanket and the tea, she seriously considered what her mother said. Iain had told her time and time again she should seek help, but to her that felt like showing she was insecure and undisciplined.

For surely, people had gone through worse during the war and now simply lived their lives. Why couldn't she?

"I promise, I'll think about seeing Doctor Finchley, Maman. Tonight, I'll discuss it with Iain. These relapses exhaust me and quite honestly scare me. But let's not talk about the war now. I'm sick of it right now. Tell me how Zack has been today. Was he not too bothered by that head cold starting up?"

Mother and daughter soon discussed every little happening of the day, especially the precious moments Lili had missed of her son's development. What he had eaten, when he had slept, with what he had played, the words he'd spoken. It was a ritual the mother and grandmother could indulge in for at least half an hour.

Lili sat straighter and her blue eyes soon shone again. As they settled for another cup of tea, she suddenly remembered another happening of the day.

"Maman, I totally forgot." Her voice bubbled with its usual enthusiasm, "I received an invitation to Le Manoir in Switzerland. Can you imagine?! After all these years, Madame Paul invites *me* back to her school. I think she must have gone soft in the head. I certainly wasn't her most favorite student."

Her mother's eyes sparkled with the mischief Lili so adored in her.

"I thought so!" Madeleine cheered, clapping her hands. "Well, that makes two of us, *ma chère*, or I should say four because Tante Agnès and Océane have also received the same invitation."

"Did you get one, too? And how do you know about Tante and Océane? Is this a conspiracy of sorts I know nothing about?" Lili giggled as she gazed at her mother.

"Non, non! I tried to phone Agnès because I was so shocked to get that letter but got Océane on the phone instead. She told me the letters had arrived in Paris as well and promised she'd phone you about it soon."

"So, are we going, Maman? With the four of us it could be fun, and we could easily parry any attacks by the Sphinx together?"

Before her mother could answer, the door flung open and little Zack raced into the room, dragging his teddy bear behind him. Molly smiled as she closed the door behind him again.

"Mummy!"

Lili let herself drop to the floor, opened her arms wide to gather her toddler son against her chest.

"Sweetheart! I missed you."

"Missed, Mummy. Daddy?"

"Yes, soon, sweetie pie."

"Daddy!" Zack cheered at the top of his lungs.

Lili felt a huge sense of contentment wash over her. Despite the challenges that lay ahead, she knew that with her family by her side, she could face anything that came her way.

And as she looked over the top of her son's dark head, the snowy landscape beyond the window gave her a glimmer of hope for a brighter future, not just for herself, but for all those she held dear.

5

OCÉANE

~ THE PARISIAN SPY ~

One day earlier - Paris, 25 January 1948

A cold January wind swept through Neuilly-sur-Seine. Streets, rooftops, treetops, and the spire of l'Église Saint-Pierre all were decked under a blanket of snow.

The white wonderland cast a serene, yet icy, atmosphere over the deserted streets. As it was past midday, the churchgoers had long since sought the warmth of their houses.

Dr. Océane Bell Riveau, her petite frame wrapped in a winter coat and thick shawl, made her way through the wintry landscape, her husband Jean-Jacques Riveau, broadly built and muscular, his blond mane without hat or cap tousled by the wind, stepping by her side. His sturdy grip on her arm provided Océane with support against the slippery pavement underfoot.

As she bent her head against the chill winds, eyes on the snow-covered path ahead, she did her best to suppress the signals of fatigue that went through her body. Her already swollen belly, a testament to the life growing inside her, seemed to weigh her down more with each passing step.

Mindful of Jean-Jacques's fussing over her well-being, Océane had learned to wave his worries away with a radiant smile, inwardly finding solace in his protective nature. But it bothered her she wasn't as swift and agile on her feet as she used to be.

"Are you alright, my dapper soldier?" He'd first called her that when as Resistance fighters they'd fought side-by-side with the Allies to liberate Paris in August 1944.

'My dapper soldier' was still Jean-Jacques's favorite pet name for her, as it represented their special bond of when they'd found each other in the final days of the war in France.

"Of course I'm alright. I could still outrun you if I needed to." She hoped her voice didn't betray her panting. Her breath formed a misty cloud in the frigid air.

Jean-Jacques squeezed her arm gently, but she saw the wrinkle of worry etch in the furrow of his brow. "We should have taken the Renault. Too much risk walking through this weather in your state."

A chuckle escaped Océane's lips as she leaned into her husband's warmth. "You know it would have taken ages to heat that old car and we still would have been frozen."

Jean-Jacques looked sheepish. "I know, I promise I'll start looking for a proper family car next week." Océane knew how attached he was to the mouse-gray Peugeot 4023 that he'd had from before the war.

Her husband had a penchant for objects that were cute and ugly at the same time and the car was one of them. Probably part of his quirky, artistic side.

It was Océane's turn to give her husband's arm a squeeze. "I agree with us buying a family car, as long as you keep your Peugeot, darling. How can I see you part with the old thing? Remember, you picked me up in it for our first date?"

"Oh, but I do, OC. How could I forget? The darn thing was giving me trouble already back then. Truly, it's silly to keep a car that's as old as the hills."

Océane shook her head. "End of discussion, JJ, the Peugeot stays." If her time as a resistance leader *and* as a physician had taught her one thing, it was to be firm when firm was needed.

They continued their journey in harmony, the crunch of snow beneath their boots the only sound for a while. Océane couldn't help but feel a sense of nostalgia as they approached her parents' home. Three generations of her family were now living in Neuilly-sur-Seine.

Her grandfather had always lived on the Boulevard in the Département Hauts-de-Seine across from the Île de la Grande Jatte, and after the war her parents had found a house nearby in the Rue Peronnet.

And now, Océane and Jean-Jacques had been lucky to find an apartment near Pont de Neuilly. The familiarity of the surroundings always offered her a comforting feeling. It was so good to have her entire family nearby, certainly after the long, lonely years of the war, when she'd often thought she'd never see them again.

As they reached the doorstep, Océane stole a glance at her husband. The worry wrinkle was still between his eyes. Despite her attempts to reassure him she was fine, it was impossible to hide anything from her artist spouse. He was eagle-eyed and finely attuned to her.

The prospect of motherhood, coupled with her demanding work at the Hôtel Dieu Hospital, seemed to loom over her like a shadow. And he knew it. Sometimes there was a limit to her toughness.

Taking a moment to gather her thoughts, she tightened her grip on Jean-Jacques's arm, drawing strength from his unshakable support. "Thank you, JJ," she whispered. "I really appreciate your always being there for me."

With a tender smile, he pressed a kiss to her forehead, his lips warm in a silent promise he'd never leave her again. And as they stepped into the warmth of her parents' home, Océane felt her heart swell. Whatever challenges may lay ahead, they would face them together.

SUNDAY FAMILY LUNCHEON at the Bell residence had become an established tradition since Agnès and Alan left Chicago in 1945 to return to Agnès's native Paris. The luncheon itself, overseen by the well-organized mistress of the house, was always an affair of timeless elegance and taste, but the dinner table conversations were often less a matter of refined control.

Put Maxipa, Océane's quirky grandfather, at the same table as her two teenage brothers and throw Madame Noir, Maxipa's never-mincing-her-words, octogenarian lover into the mix, and there were guaranteed fireworks at the table, much to the amusement of Océane and Jean-Jacques, but to the exasperation of the hosts.

Welcome kisses and admiring glances at Océane's belly were exchanged before the family took up their strategic positions at the long mahogany table at center stage in the dining room.

The table was, as usual, impeccably set with fine china and gleaming silverware, as if Agnès had indeed acquired her table setting skills under Madame Paul's tutelage. Light fell into the room through the gauze curtains in front of the tall bay windows, while candlelight from the table and sideboard cast a warm glow upon the polished silver.

Agnès, angelic yet distinguished, sat at the head of the table while her dark-haired, gray-eyed husband Alan took up his position at the other end.

Next to Agnès sat Arthur, blond and blue-eyed like his mother, in his special chair, while the other blond, blue-eyed boy, Daniel, flanked Alan's side. Océane and Jean-Jacques sat side-by-side next to Arthur, and her grandfather and his partner were seated next to Daniel on the other side of the table.

Despite his advanced years, Baron Maximilian de Dragoncourt, with his long, silvery hair combed backwards and his distinguished mustache groomed, epitomized the essence of a French, aristocratic dandy.

Adorned in silk cravats and waistcoats of the finest quality, he carried himself with an air of sophistication and refinement that belied his age.

How they had found each other in love was still their best kept secret, but Madame Noir was – at least on the exterior – the opposite of her flamboyant partner.

A figure of formidable strength and resilience, every cell of Agatha Noir's being bore the marks of her courageous past as a leader in the Paris resistance movement during the war.

Her snow-white hair served as a symbol of wisdom earned through experience, while her attire, always in mourning black, reflected the solemnity of her widowhood. Yet beneath her somber exterior lay a sharp wit and a spirited demeanor, reminiscent of the fire that fueled her defiance in the face of adversity.

The room meanwhile filled with the tantalizing aromas of French cuisine, as Agnès took great pride in serving her traditional Sunday dishes with meticulous attention to detail. The delicate bouillabaisse, fragrant with the flavors of the Mediterranean, was followed by succulent coq au vin, the rich sauce clinging to tender pieces of chicken.

Océane tried to eat but despite the tempting scents in her nostrils her stomach revolted. She put her hand protectively on her belly when she heard her grandfather exclaim, "Three esteemed doctors in our midst and they're all as blind as a bat." Maxipa opened the inevitable debate even before they'd settled into the bouillabaisse.

He threw his arms into the air, but before any of the esteemed doctors could ask what they had missed, Arthur chimed in.

"Wrong turn, Maxipa. Ba...bats aren't blind. They have small eyes with very sens... sensitive vision. They can see in pitch black. Better than humans. Our biology teacher Mademoiselle Giraffe taught us that."

"Mademoiselle Giraffe," Daniel snickered from the other side of the table. "What a fitting name for a biology teacher. Does she have a long neck?"

"Never mind," Arthur was unperturbed by his brother's interruption. Biology fascinated him. "She says you should say blind as an eye... eyeless shrimp. They only have light p... perception. Or blind as a st...star-nosed mole. A star-nosed mole is the fastest-eating m...mammal in the world. They mainly use touch as a sen... sensory organ."

"That's quite interesting, son," Alan edged in to steer the conversation back to the original topic. "Now eat your bouillabaisse before it's cold, while we hear Maxipa's diagnosis on what the doctors have collectively missed."

Océane's brown eyes fixed on Maxipa, but she saw he had forgotten he'd created a stir, or he was enjoying the build-up. One simply never knew with him. His full attention was on his plate.

But Madame Noir wouldn't have it. She simply took the spoon from his hand as it went halfway to his mouth and lay it on her own plate.

"Come on, Max, spill the beans! We're all on the edge of our seats, and I'm pretty sure the bouillabaisse is starting to feel left out in this dramatic showdown of medical expertise versus seafood. Are we about to uncover the mystery of the century, or are we just going to sit here, watching you slurp soup while we contemplate the meaning of life?"

Max chuckled, wiping his mouth with a napkin before responding, "Oh, don't rush me, Agatha. I'm just savoring the moment, relishing in the fact that for once, I'm the one holding all the cards in this game of medical charades. But fear not, my dear family, the revelation you seek is coming, and when it does, it'll be grander than the bouillabaisse itself!"

Arthur rolled his eyes, Daniel snickered, Agnès looked rather helpless, while Alan studied his father-in-law with an unreadable, but patient look on his handsome face.

Océane kicked Jean-Jacques's foot under the table, which meant *it's going to be one of these meals again.* Jean-Jacques, already used to the conversation at the Bells having the semblance of a flea circus, put his arm over his wife's chair and gave her shoulder a small squeeze.

Madame Noir meanwhile leaned back in her chair, crossing her arms with mock impatience. "Well, Max, I hope it's worth the wait. My suspense tolerance isn't what it used to be since knowing you. I might just have to start throwing bread rolls if you keep us dangling much longer."

The baron winked mischievously, enjoying the playful banter. "Oh, Agatha, you wouldn't dare waste such precious rolls on me, would you? But, my dear family, the moment of truth is approaching. You see, while you were all busy poking and prodding patients, I had my own little revelation—a nugget of wisdom that escaped even the keenest eyes of our medically-inclined family members."

Océane, fearing her grandfather would go off on another long drawn, empty speech, furrowed her dark brow. "Come on, Maxipa, enough is enough. What did you see that we missed?"

But she was in for the greatest surprise of her life. He leaned towards her, his voice dropping to a conspiratorial whisper, "Well,

my dear, it appears that you, my beloved, granddaughter doctor"—
he gestured toward her belly— "are not just carrying one bundle of
joy but two! Yes, twins, hiding in plain sight beneath that volumi-
nous lab coat you wear during the week."

Gasps erupted around the table as Océane's eyes widened in
disbelief. "Twins? Do you think? But how did you—" Suddenly the
pieces of the puzzle fell into place. Her extreme tiredness, the fast-
growing belly, but there weren't really any twins in either side of the
family. But, then again, any woman could have twins.

There was deadly silence around the table as everyone, the
doctors included, digested this news.

Arthur had it figured out first. "To form iden... identical twins,
one f...fertilised egg splits and develops two babies with exactly the
same gen...genetic information. With fra...fraternal twins two eggs
are f...fertilised by two sperm and produce two gen...genetically
unique children."

"Mademoiselle Giraffe, again?" Daniel chipped in.

"Boys, hush," Agnès admonished as she slipped from her seat
and went over to hug her daughter.

"Why do you think Océane is carrying twins, Papa?" Her voice
was as ever clear, and level-headed with just a tinge of emotion.

"Ah, *ma chère fille*, the secrets of the universe are not for me to reveal.
Let's just say a grandfather's intuition is a powerful thing," he replied
with a smug grin, taking his spoon back from his lover's plate and taking
another sip of his soup as if he'd just won the Nobel Prize for Obstetrics.

"I'll make an appointment with my obstetrician tomorrow,"
Océane remarked. "Now I want to know."

"If we have two babies instead of one, I'd be over the moon,"
Jean-Jacques remarked raising his glass to toast to the news.

"What do you think, husband?" Agnès turned to Alan, who was
smiling broadly.

"For once, I'm happy I wasn't the one having to deliver the diagnosis, but it could well be true."

Laughter and chatter filled the room once more. Amidst the clinking of glasses and the hum of conversation, the topic turned to the letter from Madame Paul of Le Manoir, its arrival stirring a lively debate among the guests. Océane, her hand resting thoughtfully on her belly, voiced her uncertainty.

"I'd love to go, if you go Mama, but the baby or babies will only be a few weeks old in June. I can hardly go. Can't leave them home but can't drag them to Switzerland either."

Her words sparked a flurry of opinions around the table, with each guest offering their own perspective on the matter.

"We can look after the babies, Mom, can't we?" Arthur suggested.

But Daniel called from the other side of the table, "hasn't Mademoiselle Giraffe taught you babies need mother milk, silly?"

Arthur looked cross, having forgotten that detail.

"I understand it's going to be a lot to consider for a new mother," Agnès, ever the voice of reason, counselled. "but, you would have me by your side and possibly Madeleine and Lili. We could rent a villa and take turns looking after the baby or babies, so you'd have some time to talk with your old friends."

Océane still looked doubtful until Jean-Jacques spoke the final word.

"I want you to honor your past, darling. I have had doubts about the exhibition in Marseille in May anyway. I'll cancel it and I'll drive you down in our new family car. And stay by your side. Would you go then?"

The smile she gave him was like the sun peeking out from behind the clouds.

"Would you do that for me, JJ?"

"I'd climb Mont Blanc and the Matterhorn in one day for you if I could, my dapper soldier. So, it's settled?"

Océane nodded when her eyes caught her grandfather's gaze from across the table. With a twinkle in his eye, he raised his glass to them, acknowledging that amidst life's uncertainties, love remains the one constant, weaving its magic through the fabric of time.

And as the meal drew to a close, he offered his simple yet profound observation, "In love, my dear family, we find both our greatest strength and our deepest joy."

In that moment, surrounded by her loved ones and filled with the warmth of camaraderie, Océane knew that despite the challenges she faced, she was blessed with a family bond that would endure through the ages.

6

ESTHER

~ THE NORWEGIAN ASSASSIN ~

Two weeks earlier - Tryvannskleiva, Norway, 12 January 1948

As the first light of dawn crept over the ski slopes of the Oslo Winter Park, casting a deep red hue over the freshly fallen snow, the Franz and Naomi Weiss Recuperation Center stood in silent anticipation.

Built with the late Franz Weiss's money – one of the 6 million Holocaust victims - the center lay nestled amidst the woods north of Oslo in the Tryvann Resort. The wooden facade blended seamlessly with the surrounding landscape, a brand-new sanctuary of solace and healing in the aftermath of Nazi-Germany's brutal war against Norway.

Esther Weiss Helberg, the unstoppable motor behind the center's existence, emerged from the warmth of her cabin, her breath forming delicate wisps in the frosty air.

Tall and straight, clad in sturdy ski attire, her blonde locks peeking out from beneath a knit cap, she stood a moment to take in the pristine silence of the early morning, listened to the low growl of a lynx claiming its territory, and studied the snow clouds drifting in from the Arctic.

There was something in the way Esther carried herself, a quiet determination born of tragedy and tempered by steely resolve, that made her at once in unison with the cold landscape around her and the master of it. A force of nature, part of nature, ruling nature, like Freya, the mythological Norse Goddess of love, beauty, youth, and fertility.

She waited until her husband, Tore, her steadfast companion in both life's joys and sorrows, joined her, carrying a rucksack with their morning coffee and breakfast.

Of imposing height and with a shock of straw-blond hair, Tore Helberg, a Norwegian resistance fighter from the first hour like his wife, shared in her mission to mend shattered spirits and rebuild fractured lives at the family's center.

"Ready for the competition, *Jeger*?" he asked. Esther nodded. 'Jeger,' meaning 'hunter,' had been her code name during the war, and Tore loved using it just before they embarked on their early morning routine.

Who would beat whom down the slope today? Tore pressed a kiss on his wife's warm lips, which she answered with a grin before donning her helmet and ski goggles.

The skiing routine was their fun competitive start to the day. Tore had been with the Norwegian National Skiing Team before the war and Esther had traversed the Austrian Alps on skis since she was in diapers.

Both formidable skiers, the first few hundred yards they'd glide down their private slope side-by-side, their movements fluid and graceful in total sync.

Esther loved how the snow beneath their skis whispered tales of resilience and survival, each crystalline flake a testament to the enduring spirit of those who had faced the horrors of the death camps but had emerged, scarred yet undefeated. For the slope was both a source of therapy and of healing. Even for her. Every single day.

She was the one to give the signal. Accelerating as they passed the tall pine tree to the left of them. It was an even race for most of the track, as they knew every nuance of each other's strength and weakness, but neither had mercy with the other.

Esther glanced sideways. She'd gained a ski length on Tore and was adamant to keep her first-place position. But there was something, a small flutter in her belly that made her hold back from giving it every ounce of her strength.

She gave what she reasonably could, as she did every day, but Tore had gained half a ski-length, three-quarters, was level with her... and overtook her. He won, and now it was three days in a row she'd lost.

"Tomorrow, I'll win!" She stabbed her ski pole in the snow with intensity, her cheeks red, her eyes ablaze. Esther hated losing.

"You do that, *Jeger*, unless I don't let you," Tore smiled. "But for today, the race is over and you have earned your coffee and a thick slice of the sunnmørsbrød I baked especially for you."

They sat down on a log at the foot of the slope while the bright January sun rose over the mountain peaks. Esther took off her helmet, shook her hair loose and accepted the tin mug with steaming coffee and the succulent sandwich with fresh goat cheese.

They ate in silence, enjoying the unspoiled nature around them, the feeling of having stretched their limbs, and the knowledge of understanding each other's hearts without words.

Esther squinted her eyes against the sun and looked up from where they'd come. In the distance, the therapy wing of the center stood as a beacon of hope, its windows aglow in the bright sunlight.

"Isn't it amazing Dr Wiesenthal will be joining us today?" she observed after having finished her hearty breakfast. Chaim Wiesenthal, himself a camp survivor and esteemed psychiatrist, had been pivotal in the first treatments of Esther's sister Sarah.

Though the doctor had recently opened a new clinic in London, he'd offered to work with them for a month to establish the new center and treat the first patients himself. Esther and Tore were responsible for the housing facilities, physical training, and the dietary parts of the therapy.

"It is, darling. A testament to your charm and perseverance I'd say." Tore closed the breakfast boxes and screwed the lid on the thermos.

Esther agreed. It had been a daunting and unusual project to create a Jewish rehabilitation center so far away from Germany and Austria, where the horrors had taken place, but Doctor Wiesenthal had backed her plans from the beginning.

"I'm sure that fresh air, exercise, and diet, in combination with trauma therapy by a team of professionals, is the best offer there is to promote healing. And your passion, Esther Weiss. Remember, I told you to follow your passion when you just learned you'd lost your brother, your father, your mother, your aunt, and your fiancé to the murderous Nazis. And your only remaining family member was too heavily traumatized to meet you. The last emotion you wanted was passion. And yet, it was the answer."

"Despite Doctor Wiesenthal's encouragement, I'm nervous," Esther acknowledged, rising to her feet, and stamping the snow from her boots. "I truly hope the first five patients he brings with him will not find the Franz and Naomi Weiss Recuperation Center a waste of their time."

"I'm sure they won't, darling." Tore rose as well. He slung the rucksack on his back and threw his long arms around her. "You look a bit pale today. Don't worry too much. I'm sure today will work out well, but I understand this is a big day for you. Come on, let's get to the ski lift and get ready for our official first day of work together."

As Esther and Tore guided their skis towards the heart of the center, the snow-capped peaks loomed overhead like silent sentinels, guardians of a landscape scarred by history, yet resplendent with the promise of renewal.

"Oh, I almost forgot," Esther said as they sat huddled together in the lift that would take them back up the mountain. "I got an unexpected letter from Switzerland. Do you remember I once told you I went there to a finishing school in 1938, just after Hitler had annexed Austria?"

"Of course, I remember," Tore squeezed her hand. "How could I forget? You told me how Carl took you to the train on the Swiss border and that was the very last you ever saw of him."

Esther swallowed. It took a man of Tore's caliber to pay tribute to Carl Bernstein, her first fiancé, the kind-hearted jeweler who'd stayed behind in Vienna to look after his ageing parents and who'd died in Dachau in the summer of 1944 in the presence of his childhood friend Ash Hoffmann, now Edda's husband.

Yes, it took a man of Tore's caliber to never pass over his wife's past but embrace every aspect of it, no matter how hard, how brutal, how devastating. He was with her every step of the way, like a giant shadow but made of light.

Esther's heart swelled as she gazed up at that robust profile with the chiseled jawline, those ice-blue Nordic eyes. Another flutter went through her tummy, as if squeezing something from within.

"What's with the letter?" he asked.

"Oh yes, the letter. The headmistress, a Jew-hater named Madame Paul, asked if I'd like to come to her 30th anniversary celebration of running the school."

Tore laughed. "You don't make the invitation sound very enticing. I guess you're not going?'

Esther laughed with him. "No, I never imagined I'd ever hear of Madame Paul again, let alone hear *from* her, and had totally forgotten her existence. But my God, did I try my best at that school, Tore. You should have seen the diligent me, immersed in setting the perfect table and making the prettiest flower arrangement. I was still totally expecting to run a grand house in Vienna and mix in high society there. Ball after soiree after luncheon." Esther laughed again, gazing down at her practical ski outfit under which hid a commando-trained body.

"When's the anniversary ceremony?" Tore was looking at her with that thoughtful look on his face.

"Why?" Esther shrugged, "I'm not going."

"Shouldn't you ask the other girls if they have been invited too? You thoroughly enjoyed spending a weekend in Paris last year with Lili and Océane..."

"That's different. Like us visiting Edda and Ash in Amsterdam and corresponding with Sable and Anna. We talk more about the war than silly Le Manoir. I'm sure that if they also got an invitation, they're not going. Besides I have a center to run. I can't travel this year."

Tore was still fixing her with that unflappable gaze, just how he'd gazed at her when they'd first laid eyes on each other.

She with a cup of tea on the day of her engagement to Carl, staring through the window of Himmlhof Inn in the Austrian Alps. He skiing down the Radstädter Tauern Pass at full speed. February 1938. It had been the first time they'd tested each other's strength. Esther gave in.

"Alright. I'll contact the girls and see what they say."

"Good, Jeger. Let me know."

"But not before the weekend," Esther added quickly.

Amidst the embrace of the mountains and the crisp winter air, Esther again felt how sorrow and hope converged in a timeless dance. Le Manoir. *That* Esther. That hopeful, sweet girl. She'd come such a long way. Such a long, lonely way.

Her heart was full when she put the key in the door to the Franz and Naomi Weiss Recuperation Center.

"Esther?"

She turned around. Tore stood, his tall posture barring the sunlight, the straw mane aflame like a halo.

"Yes?"

He didn't say anything. Just stood there, ready to bring their breakfast gear to the cabin before starting lunch for their guests.

"I love you, Esther, and I have tremendous respect for you."

"I love you too, Tore."

And with these words Esther stepped into her new role as head of the center that connected her past to her future.

7

SABLE

~ THE HIGHLAND RAVEN ~

Alnor Castle, Scottish Highlands, 15 January 1948

The morning mist clung to the turrets of Alnor Castle, veiling the grandeur of its ancient stone walls in an ethereal shroud, as a giant cake dusted with white, powdery icing.

A thick layer of frost glistened on the grassy grounds, and the breath of the cold Scottish air danced in tendrils around the estate.

Against this wintry backdrop, the castle stood as a testament to centuries of Montgomery history, its imposing Neo-Gothic presence softened by the gentle brush strokes taken from nature's winter palette.

It was a magical morning in the Highlands but way too cold for people and animals to venture out-of-doors.

Within the castle walls, the morning room was a buzz of activity with the breakfast table set with all the elegance befitting its aristocratic inhabitants.

Lady Sable Montgomery Mitchell, her raven-black hair

cascading in a long ponytail down her slender back, sat at the head of the table, her piercing, light blue eyes alive with anticipation.

"Wild Bill", her rugged husband with his fiery red hair and beard, occupied the seat opposite her, his reddish brows furrowed in thought, as he jotted down some words in an earmarked notebook.

Isabella, their 11-year-old daughter, a blonde, blue-eyed nymph who looked nothing like either of her parents, bubbled with excitement, her starry-eyed gaze fixed on her mother as she eagerly cried out.

"Mummy darling, isn't it time for me to wear my hair like you, in a ponytail instead of in these childish braids. I'm eleven-and-a-half now. Prissy says…"

"Your eleven and three weeks, sweetheart. That's a big difference," Sable smiled at her precocious daughter. Isabella was, and always would be, quite a handful, in every way so much ahead of her age. The fight over the braids had started as soon as she turned eleven on the 25th of December.

"But Mummy dear, your hair looks positively adorable. Don't you think so too, Daddy?"

"Huh, what was that?" Bill looked up from his scribbling, the blue gaze under the hairy brows going from his wife to his adopted daughter.

"My hair, Daddy. *This* is that," Isabella said as she held up her two long braids on each side of her ears and looked dramatically unhappy. "Even Uncle Freddy says braids are for babies. Well, do you, Mother and Father, still consider me a baby? If so, I think it's time you two had a real baby and let me wear my hair in a ponytail."

She looked triumphant, while her mother suppressed a grin and her father looked lost. He was clearly more in tune with Shakespeare that morning than with his sharp-witted daughter.

"Well, Daddy. What is your verdict? Do you prefer Mummy's hair or mine?"

But before he could answer, Sable had taken the tie from her hair and divided it in two strands on either side of her head. With swift, nimble fingers she braided her hair and tied both ends together with the hair tie.

"There," she declared, "now leave your dad alone. He's perfectly content to have two ladies with braids."

For a moment Isabella gazed at her mother with a stunned expression on her face, but then she exploded with laughter, clapping her hand over her mouth to suppress her glee.

"Mummy looks like a pirate!"

"Eat your porridge before it gets cold, little buccaneer, or you'll be swabbing the decks!"

For a moment there was silence at the table, until Sable's voice cut through the stillness like a clarion call. "Darlings," she began, her own tone now carrying a hint of excitement, "I have the most extraordinary news to share with you."

Bill raised a skeptical eyebrow, his gaze fixed on his wife. "And what might that be, my dear?" he inquired, his voice tinged with a mixture of curiosity and concern. He was well-aware that both his women were exuberantly energetic.

Sable smiled, her eyes sparkling with anticipation. "It seems Winston Churchill himself has requested my presence in Paris!" she announced, her voice now filled with pride. "He wishes for me to serve as the ambassador to the UK, representing our nation in the heart of France."

Isabella gasped in delight, her eyes widening with excitement. "Paris?" she exclaimed, "Like Paris, the capital of France?" Her voice went up another octave. "Oh, Mummy, can we truly go? It sounds positively magical! We must! We must!"

Bill's expression darkened as he digested this unexpected news.

"But Sable ye've only been the MP for the Westminster Constituency for two years. Don't ye think it's too early? Some more years of experience in the House of Commons first?" Bill was clearly mulling over the implications of such a sudden career move.

Sable's clear eyes found those of her husband over the table. Isabella wisely held her mouth. This was going to be an adult decision and she watched the tug of war with keen interest.

"Exactly my first thought, darling," Sable acknowledged,. "That's why I've been brooding over this news since the letter arrived yesterday."

She looked torn, a wrinkle clouding her otherwise smooth forehead. "Maybe I shouldn't have brought the matter up at the breakfast table." Her eyes darted to Cuthbert "Killer" Drake and Johnny "Lock" Clark, two weathered veterans from Sable's former life as an SOE agent, who were now employed at Alnor. "We can talk about it in private, Bill."

"Never mind, *Mo Chridhe,* it's out in the open now. And it's a grand opportunity, to be sure," he conceded, but Sable could hear the uncertainty in his voice.

"What else is there, Bill? I want to know what you think."

"Apart from yer work in London, what about our responsibilities here in Scotland? And what of my work as a poet? The Highlands are where my muse resides, after all. Ye know that."

Sable's gaze softened with understanding. "I know, my love," she murmured, her voice filled with empathy. "There's a lot to think about, but it's also a once in a lifetime opportunity for me to become the Ambassador to the UK in France. I gave so much for that country."

Her eyes filled with tears at the thought of how narrowly she'd escaped after her arrest by the Gestapo and how many of her friends, like Irish Maureen Knight and Dutch Egbert Van Eijck, had never returned and found early graves in German concentration camps.

She wiped her tears away with her napkin, frustrated at her own weakness. Sable hated weakness and hated the war getting to her, yet it happened at unexpected times. Like now.

Bill had risen from his chair and taken a seat next to her, putting his arm around her. Isabella stared at her empty plate, her own eyes brimming over with tears, though she had no idea why. She just got sad if Mummy got sad. Sadness and happiness in Isabella had gone up and down according to her mother's emotions since the two of them had been reunited after the war.

"Maybe ask Freddie's opinion?" Bill suggested, softly rubbing Sable's back. "He's always a good advisor." But Sable shook her head. It was true she was very close with her half-brother Freddie, but Freddie wasn't the one who would go with her to Paris. This was a family affair.

"I think it would be a great adventure for the three of us," she observed, her voice gaining steadiness again, "but I don't want to take you away from Scotland, Bill. As far as your concerns about Alnor, we now have Cuthbert and Johnny to help manage the estate in our absence. And we would return every holiday."

At the mention of their names, the former SOE instructors nodded solemnly from their places at the table. Though their days of espionage were behind them, their loyalty to Sable remained steadfast, a silent testament to the bonds forged in the crucible of war.

Bill's hand fell still on her back. He seemed to consider the new adventure in all earnest. "*Mo Chridhe*, I want ye to do what ye're good at above all. I know yer ambition. Ye want a career in politics and diplomacy with every fiber of yer bein'. Ye're so much yer father's daughter and he would have been so proud of ye."

Unable to stay silent any longer, Isabella seized upon her father's words with renewed enthusiasm. "Oh, please, Mummy, Daddy, does that mean we are going?!" she pleaded, her eyes shining with excitement. "I'm sure you will find even more inspiration at the paths along the Seine, Daddy. Plus, I simply cannot bear the thought of missing out on such a grand adventure! You must think of me as well, Mummy and Daddy."

Her father chuckled at his daughter's exuberance, his heart warmed by her infectious enthusiasm. "Very well, my dear," he conceded, his gaze meeting Sable's with a mixture of resolve and affection. "If Paris is where my ladies' hearts truly lie, then Paris it shall be."

"Thank you, darling, thank you for always considering my needs." Sable planted a kiss on her husband's bearded cheek, then laughed out loud.

"Something else!" she snorted, "I got another letter as well. The weirdest invitation I've ever received."

"Another letter?" Isabella rolled her eyes. This was going to be a long breakfast.

The morning sunlight started to filter through the curtains, casting a warm glow over the breakfast table.

"Can we be excused, Ma'am, Sir? We've got work to do," Cuthbert announced as he and Johnny raised up from the table, clearly feeling this was going to be another family affair.

Sable rose as well, wagging her finger. "No!" she reprimanded, "for heaven's sake, we've gone over this a million times, Killer and Lock. We are Sable and Bill. If you can't say our Christian names, call us Bable and Sill for all I care, but stop Ma'am-ing and Sir-ing."

Everyone laughed.

"Alright, Bable and Sill," Johnny cheered, "we've got the message. Now release us from breakfast prison, please."

After the men left, Sable sat down again with her husband and daughter. The aroma of freshly brewed coffee mingled with the scent of buttered toast, creating a cozy atmosphere in the antique dining room.

Sable retrieved a crumpled piece of paper from the pocket of her pants and flattened it on the table, the crest of Le Manoir clearly stamped on top of the letter.

"What is it, Mummy?" Isabella asked, her youthful eagerness evident in her voice.

Sable took a moment to compose herself before continuing. "I've received an invitation to the 30th anniversary of Madame Paul at Le Manoir."

There was a moment of silence around the table as Bill and Isabella processed Sable's words. Isabella's eyes widened in surprise, while Bill's expression remained unreadable.

"What is Le Manoir?" Isabella implored, "It sounds like a stable for racehorses."

"Le Manoir?" Bill repeated with a tinge of disbelief in his voice. "But... didn't you have a rather...unpleasant experience there?"

Sable nodded, her gaze dropping to her hands as she remembered the events that had led to her expulsion from the prestigious Swiss school.

"Yes," she admitted. "I was expelled in 1939... after a skiing trip."

"What is Le Manoir, though?" Isabella had figured out it had nothing to do with racehorses but rather skiing.

"It was a finishing school in Switzerland where I went before the war. After...," Sable hesitated, "... after you were taken away from me, Isabella, and I was sick with grief and full of rebellion."

Isabella sensed new tears threatening to well up, so she slid from her chair to sit close to her mother, leaning into her. Sable drew her daughter onto her lap and though eleven years and one month, Isabella didn't protest but sat very still against her mother's chest.

"What happened Mummy?" she asked in a small voice, feeling the tension hang in the air.

Sable took a deep breath, gathering her thoughts before recounting the events of that fateful night on the slopes of St Moritz.

She spoke of her reckless behavior, the accident in the dark, the hospitalization, and the subsequent expulsion from the school.

"But," she added with a feeling of gratitude, "Océane and Esther... they saved me. And I was so happy to meet up with Esther in Shetland in 1941."

"Esther, like in Auntie Esther?" Isabella interrupted. "Esther who helped me look for your rings after they dropped from the velvet cushion and rolled all through the church? When you and Daddy got married?"

"Yes, your Auntie Esther."

"I love Auntie Esther! And she has the prettiest hair. I love Uncle Tore as well, though he looks a bit like a Viking," Isabella rattled on. Her daughter's reminiscing gave Sable time to collect her thoughts and to also feel a warmth for Esther and Tore spread through her. They'd been at Bill and her wedding in the spring of 1946 and in turn Sable and Bill had flown to Oslo for Esther and Tore's wedding three months ago.

"So, what will ye do, my darlin'?" Bill broke the silence. "Is there any part of ye that would like to return to that school?"

Sable glanced up, meeting her husband's concerned gaze. "I'm not sure," she admitted. "I think...I'll consult with Esther first, see if she's received the invitation as well. Madame Paul says something about wanting to honor the batch of girls, us, who were in the Resistance. Which, to be honest, is rather hypocritical as I remember her being an antisemite and any mention of 'war' or 'Hitler' was as strictly forbidden as making music after dinner."

"Why no music after dinner?" Isabella looked puzzled.

"Never mind, dear. It was a strange school during strange times. That's all."

Bill nodded. "I think it's a good idea to see what Esther says," he observed. "Anyway, when's the happy occasion?"

"In June. I have no idea whether we'll be in Paris by that time or not."

"Isn't Océane also in Paris?" Bill asked.

"Correct. I could contact her too."

"We'll support you whatever you decide." Bill rose from the table, ready to get to work.

Isabella smiled reassuringly at her mother. "Yes, Mummy," she mimicked in her grown-up voice. "We'll be here for you no matter what."

"Thank you, darlings." Sable smiled at her loving duo.

"Oh, one more thing," Isabella remarked. "When you go to your finishing school, can I go and stay with Uncle Freddie and Uncle David? They're going to buy a new plane and I want them to fly me over the Alps so I can wave at you."

"We'll see about that, honey."

With the love and support of her family behind her, Sable felt a sense of reassurance wash over her, a glimmer of hope that perhaps attending the reunion would provide an opportunity for closure - a chance to reconcile with her past and truly embrace the future.

8

EDDA

~ THE CRYSTAL BUTTERFLY ~

Amsterdam, 15 January 1948

Edda Valkena Hoffmann stood at the heart of the bustling room in their Vondelstraat residence, her dark eyes alight with joy as she cradled her newborn daughter, Adina Olga Rita Hoffmann against her chest.

The warmth of the hearth mingled with the laughter and chatter of dear friends and family, who had gathered to celebrate the newest addition to their family.

"Isn't she just perfect?" Edda exclaimed, her voice filled with pride as she glanced up at her husband, Asher, who stood beside her.

"She's more than perfect, my love. She is the mini version of you, my butterfly girl," Asher replied, his eyes shining with adoration as he reached out to gently touch their daughter's tiny hand. The little fist immediately opened and firmly gripped his index finger.

It was a moment etched in time, two beautiful ballet dancers, their bodies toned, their minds full of parenting, and their souls unified in this tiny infant.

Familiar faces mingled around the luminous couple. Doctor Maarten van Lanschot, a fellow resistance fighter from Edda's war days, clasped her free hand warmly in congratulations. "She's a true miracle, Edda. You both are," he said, his voice tinged with emotion.

"Thank you again for assisting with the delivery," Edda beamed. "Thanks to your simple instructions it was a breeze."

"Not really," Asher and Maarten grinned in unison, but Maarten added with more seriousness. "It was that you insisted you wanted a home delivery and that I'd be at your side, Edda. I'm sure our dear friend Doctor Geuze over there would have been adamant that as an orthopaedic physician I should've stuck to deformed bones and muscles."

"Then don't tell him," Edda put her finger to her lips. "Can you hold Addey for a bit, Ash? So many people are entering at once, I should go and greet them. Or should we put her in her cot? She's fast asleep." But Edda needn't ask.

"No, no, give her to me. People will want to admire her. But don't tire yourself, darling. Sit down if you need to." Ash's dark head was already bowing over the angelic little face, kissing the tiny brow, while he gently shifted the little bundle into his strong arms.

From the day Addey was born, two weeks earlier on the 1st of January - as if to personally herald the new year - Ash had shown a fierce protection of his baby daughter, and he seemed even more attentive to her little cries and suckling sounds than Edda.

Being a mother not only had been a huge change for her, but Edda had also watched in amazement the transformation that had taken place in Ash. As if he was whole again, as whole as he would ever be, and her heart swelled at thought of this gentle giant with the body of a god and the heart of a lion.

They shared a deep smile, warm as an embrace, before Edda

moved away, elegant as ever in a simple, dark-green, afternoon dress, her dark curly hair piled high on top of her beautiful head, for once not glued to her skull like when performing on stage but styled with a looseness that accented her beauty even further.

Duifje Sipkema, Edda's half-sister, stood nearby with her children Benny and Elly, their laughter ringing through the room. Duifje, blond and tall, her clothes always looking a tad too big on her bony body, exclaimed, "I can't believe how quickly she's grown since last week."

Duifje's light eyes, so much like their late father's, who the girls shared as common parent, brimmed with affection as she gazed at her niece.

"Let me know if I need to give Corrie any help, Edda. So many cups of coffee and cake to serve."

Elly, now a sprightly girl of eight and, as always, dressed in her tutu as if she was about to go to her ballet class, chimed in. "I can help Corrie, Tante Edda. Please can I help, Mama?"

The sisters looked at each other. "Sure," they replied in unison. And Elly danced away to the kitchen like a happy bunny.

"So, how's it being back in Amsterdam after your time in New York?" Duifje asked, hugging her cardigan around her, and watching her younger sister. Edda and Ash had taken the opportunity to live in New York for two years after the war to give their dance career a boost.

"Honestly?" A tiny but happy smile lingered around Edda's lips, "It's heaven. New York was not our place. The work was great and I've very grateful we were given the opportunity to dance with the New York City Ballet, but we were quite lonely at times. Of course, we had each other but, still..."

"You're not saying you missed me, Lientje?" Duifje put an arm around her sister and Edda leaned into her. Lientje, Duifje's pet name for her when they were younger. She loved the sound of it.

"I did, Duif. And I also missed Valkena Estate. I can't wait to take Addey to Friesland with us."

"Wait till the weather gets better, hun. It was quite a slippery drive down. But everything is fine at your estate, Mrs. Marchioness. Jan's the best estate manager in the world. You'll see."

"And a great husband, I assume?" Edda inquired.

"Nothing to complain about there either," Duifje smirked. "But hey, don't let me keep you. You and I have plenty of time to catch up now you're back. Go and talk to your other guests and I'll help Elly with that plate of cakes before they all land on the floor." And turning to her eleven-year-old son, Bennie, who stood a little forlorn in the room, Duifje said, "Why don't you play us some tunes on the piano, Ben? Not too loud but just like some background sound."

"May I, Tante Edda?" His eyes, very much like his deceased father Teppo, regained their cheerful glance.

"Of course, Virtuoso! We love it when you play the piano."

After a quick glance at her daughter and husband, who still stood beaming in the middle of the room, Edda made her way to her once dance-rival-turned-dear-friend, Maria Petrova.

Maria had brought a man with her, of whom Edda had heard much but had never met. The famous surrealist painter and resistance fighter, Pierre Bosch van Rosenthal.

"Masha, darling," Edda greeted her, "I'm so curious..." but Maria interrupted her.

"Fie, Edda, you've been on your feet way too long. Yes, I've been watching you! If you ever want to steal my fire again in The Nutcracker, you'd better sit down and give your mama body some rest."

Without further ado, Maria grabbed Edda with one hand and her boyfriend with the other and directed them to the comfy sofa in the back room.

The energetic Russian didn't rest until Edda was propped up

against the cushions with her legs on a footstool. The sliding doors were open ensuring Ash and Addey were never out of Edda's eyesight.

"Now, tea!" Masha commanded. "Would you, Pierre?"

It was the first time Edda heard Pierre talk. The handshake had been firm but only accompanied by a short nod.

"Sure. Sugar, milk?" A posh accent for such a grizzly looking man.

"Both please," Maria and Edda replied in unison.

"So where did you two meet?" Edda asked as soon as Pierre had turned his back on them. Bosch von Rosenthal was a tall, lean man with a striking presence centered around piercing, blue eyes that seemed to hold a depth of emotion and intellect.

His aristocratic lineage, was evident to Edda in his refined features, yet there was a rebellious glint in his eyes that suggested a nonconformist spirit. Edda quickly added, "By the way, he's gorgeous."

"He's a dear," Maria laughed leaning back in the cushions next to Edda and taking her hand in hers. "But Pierre's a complicated man. Which I adore. I hate open-book characters. And I love his hair!"

Edda let her eyes wander to Pierre as he stood talking to Corrie, her housekeeper. She had to admit she'd never seen a man wear his hair this long. It fell halfway down his back in a tousled disarray, probably mirroring the chaotic beauty of his surrealist paintings.

Maria continued, "we met at Marlene and Sergeyev's. Pierre's been a family friend for years. He was an organiser in the Dutch Resistance, but I suppose you knew that?"

"Yes," Edda agreed, "big name indeed. Saved hundreds of Jews by hiding them all over the country."

At the mention of their former teachers, both Edda's and Maria's eyes darted to Miss Marlene Sterling and Monsieur Sergeyev who'd just come in and stood admiring little Addey and congratulating Ash. Edda made as if to get up and welcome them, but Maria held her back.

"Let them come to you, darling. You must rest and drink your tea first or you'll have to find a wet nurse for that little urchin of yours."

"Thank you, Masha. I wouldn't know what to do without you. We've gone through so much together, haven't we?"

"We have, my darling, we have indeed. I'm so happy you're back in Amsterdam. And little Addey, she's absolutely beautiful."

At that moment, Edda finally felt relaxation envelope her, being in the midst of her family and friends. It was Maria's Russian-accented voice, adding a touch of warmth to her words, that made Edda drift back to that day in 1944 when she'd lost consciousness due to a high fever and Maria had shown up at her bedside and nursed her back to health.

"Thank you, Masha," Edda cast her friend a big smile. "I couldn't have made it through without you."

Miss Sterling and Mr. Sergeyev still stood with Ash, admiring the baby, and chatting with him. They turned to look for Edda and soon came over to her. Their proud smiles were a testament to the talent they'd nurtured in their protégé and which had resulted in such triumph over tragedy.

"We always knew you were destined for greatness, Edda. But this tops it all, doesn't it?" A warm kiss landed on Edda's cheek, and her cheeks blushed with happiness and a tinge of tiredness. Mr. Sergeyev pressed her shoulder as he used to do, an encouraging and appreciative gesture.

"*Félicitations, ma chère Edda!*"

But amidst the joy and laughter, a shadow lingered in Edda's mind, and she was glad Miss Sterling sat down beside her so she could discuss the matter with her. Since her mother's passing, but even long before that, Miss Sterling had been Edda's trusted confidant and mentor.

"Do you have a moment, Miss Sterling? I would like to discuss something with you?"

"I have all the time of the world, silly girl. I'm here for you and for Ash of course. But please drop the 'miss' and call me Marlene. And that man over there is called Pjotr. Understood? It's time we forgo these formalities and treat each other as equals. So, what's up?"

"Oh, nothing serious. Just something I'd like your opinion on. I received a letter from the finishing school I went to, you know... when I broke my foot..." Edda glanced over at Maria, who had skipped over to Pierre and stood talking with him in that intimate way only lovers do.

"Yes, I remember you travelled to Switzerland with your mother. Lausanne, was it?"

"Yes. The school's called Le Manoir. Thankfully, I only had to stay for a short while because my leg healed quickly. Madame Paul wasn't a very pleasant headmistress, and the curriculum wasn't really my thing. All I wanted was to get back to dancing."

"So, has she passed or what, that Madame Paul?"

"Oh no, she invited me to her 30th anniversary. It is in June, so Addey will be a bit bigger by then, but I wondered if you think it's worth the effort to go there."

"If you don't really have fond memories, I doubt it's worth the trip, Edda."

"But..." Edda's brow furrowed with uncertainty. "She's organizing a special ceremony for our cohort. Because most of us joined the Resistance in our own countries. At least, there was something about that in the letter."

Marlene's honey eyes fixed on Edda. "Are you thinking about your friend Esther?"

Edda nodded. "I'll ask her. She may also have had the invitation. And Esther was friends with Lili and Océane. I wouldn't mind seeing them again. They were nice. And there was an English girl with a German accent, Anna. She was alright as well. I just didn't care much for a girl called Sable, but we've all grown in the war I guess."

Marlene was silent for a while, then said in her posh British voice, "I get a feeling you'd actually like to go, Edda-girl. Maybe Ash wouldn't mind either. After all, he recuperated in Switzerland after his ordeal in the concentration camps. Make it a family vacation?"

"Oh, I hadn't even thought of that. That's a great idea." Edda felt a lot lighter having discussed this complicated page from her past with the right person. Ash came in carrying Addey, who was waking up and making sucking sounds.

"This one is looking for her mama," he smiled.

As Edda looked down at her daughter's innocent face with the deep, dark eyes that sought her own, a surge of love and determination filled the young mother's heart.

Whatever lay ahead, she would face it with courage and conviction. For her daughter was the embodiment of hope, a beacon of light in a world still scarred by darkness.

The scent of coffee, brandy, and firewood drifted through the air, mingling with the sound of laughter and music that filled the room. Outside, the snow continued to fall, blanketing the Dutch capital in a quiet embrace.

But within those walls, there was warmth and love, a testament to the resilience of the human spirit in the face of adversity.

And as Edda held her daughter close, she knew that no matter what the future held, they would face it together, with hearts full of hope and hands clasped in solidarity.

9

ANNA

~ THE LONDON SPYMAKER ~

London, 15 January 1948

Large snowflakes danced in the frosty air, whirling down from an invisible sky and covering all of London under a winter's blanket.

A lonely robin landed on a tree branch, picking at the snow in search of food, its red breast the only color in a completely white world.

In the charming, red-brick Victorian building off Flood Street, Anna Adams Pilecki sat at her desk in the bay window surrounded by stacks of papers and files, the remnants of her tireless pursuit for justice.

The room was alight with the soft glow of two lamps, their light casting a halo over Anna's bowed dark head. The scent of Earl Grey tea lingered in the air, mingling with the faint aroma of ink from the fountain pen she held in her hand.

With a heavy sigh and pushing her glasses up her nose, Anna

lifted the receiver of the rotary telephone on her desk, her fingers dialing a familiar number.

As she waited for the line to connect, her gaze drifted to the black-and-white photograph on the wall opposite her—a group portrait of the female SOE agents she'd recruited and sent into the heart of occupied France. Taken sometime in 1943.

Her friend Pearl, as always, the shining center of the group. five years seemed decades ago.

As memories of those turbulent times flooded Anna's mind, each face in the photograph remained a testament to bravery and sacrifice. Of the nine young women smiling into the camera, proudly posing in their WAAF uniforms, only two had returned.

"Hello?" A voice sounded through the line, and Anna straightened in her chair, composing herself.

"Sable, it's Anna," she said, her voice soft but resolute. "I hope I'm not interrupting anything?"

There was a brief pause before Sable's voice responded, tinged with the warmth and familiarity that had grown between the two women since the war. "Anna, darling! It's been too long. How are you holding up? I was just thinking of you the other day."

Anna's lips curved into a weary smile. "Were you, now? What a coincidence. I'm still busy as ever, I'm afraid. You know me, I can't let go, not even when I should. But I wanted to share something with you, if you have time."

"Of course, all the time in the world for you," Sable's clear voice sounded with the greatest sincerity.

Anna hesitated, grappling with the weight of the words she was about to speak. "I've received some troubling information about Andrée Kahn. It seems... she may not have met her end at Natzweiler Struthof, as we initially believed." As Anna spoke the words, her gaze was fixed on the black-haired Indian beauty with her distinct unibrow eyebrows in the photograph on the wall.

Sable's gasp echoed through the line, and Anna could almost see the shock reflected in her friend's eyes. "But that's impossible, Anna! You said Brian Stonehouse was certain he'd seen her. Didn't he draw An—"

"Brian, apparently, was mistaken," Anna gently interrupted. "Not his fault. The woman he saw walking to the barracks at Natzweiler must have looked like Andrée. But her trail leads elsewhere, to Dachau. I'm still trying to find out who it was that Brian saw. Perhaps not one of our agents, but an - as yet - unknown French resistance fighter."

There was a heavy silence, broken only by the soft ticking of the clock on Anna's desk. She could almost feel the weight of Sable's emotions on the other side of the line.

Sable and Andrée had been so close, first coming from the same training cohort and then both working together for the Papillon Network in Lyon.

"So where does the Dachau trail come from? And what can I do for you?" Sable finally said, her voice firmer. "We owe it to Andrée and her family to uncover the truth."

"I received a letter from Fraulein Backer, who used to be one of the decent wardens in the ordinary *Frauengefängnis* in Karlsruhe and whom I interviewed in 1946. She told me that some of the female agents were temporarily held at Akademiestrasse 11 before being sent to a concentration camp."

"That was how you found out about Maureen,Madeleine, and Yvonne, right?" Sable asked.

"Indeed," Anna said with a sigh. "So, in her letter, Fraulein Backer apologized that she'd suddenly remembered there had been another prisoner, kept in a special cell with chains on her feet because she was a known flight risk. Her description of this agent sounded so like Andrée that I phoned Fraulein Backer to get more details. Everything she could remember from the short period she was held there was spot on. Dark-hair, olive skin, slight but tall, big, brown eyes, unibrow, incredibly resilient, wouldn't talk but endlessly sang French songs or recited the Bhagavat Gita... No other agent knew the Hindu scripture."

"Oh no," Sable moaned. "We knew she wouldn't return but this...this is another blow to her family. To have thought she died somewhere else."

"I know," Anna sympathized. "I feel so bad about telling the Khan family the wrong information, and having another mystery to solve. Who had been the fourth female victim in Natzweiler Struthof? Her family needs closure as well, even if it wasn't one of our agents."

"Anna, darling!" Sable sounded authoritarian, as Anna knew her friend could be. "At some point you must drop your war investigations and start living again. For Heaven's sake you have an amazingly patient husband and an adorable daughter. Focus on them, focus on your future."

Relief flooded through Anna, mingling with a sense of gratitude for her friend's support. "You're right, Sable. Just this one last case and I'll close the investigation. I promise."

"I'm going to hold you accountable to that, my dear," Sable laughed.

"You do that. Oh, and one more thing, Sable. I was wondering if you also got Madame Paul's invitation to come to her anniversary in June?"

"I was waiting for a moment to bring it up but wasn't sure it befitted our serious conversation," Sable remarked "So yes, even I got the letter, haha, but I can't say anything definitive about going or not. Plans are a bit up in the air in the Montgomery Mitchell household at the moment."

"I thought there would not be one hair on your head that considered going, Sable," Anna giggled. "Le Manoir was not a great experience for either of us, but your expulsion topped it all."

"If you go, Anna, I'll seriously consider going too. If my schedule permits it," Sable promised. "Might be fun to see the other girls. We need to find out if they're willing to go."

"True."

As they exchanged a few more words on the invitation, Anna's attention was drawn to the sound of the door opening, followed by the soft murmur of Henryk's voice.

She glanced up to see him standing in the doorway, a warm smile on his face as he cradled their daughter in his arms.

"I have to go, Sable," Anna said quickly, her heart swelling with love at the sight of her family. "Talk to you soon."

With a final farewell, Anna hung up the phone, her thoughts already turning to the next step in her investigation. But as she watched Henryk and Sarah stand waiting for her to go to the park with them, a sense of peace washed over her—a reminder that, no matter the final hurdle that she faced, she had a loving family that kept her sane and with two feet on the ground.

Eagerly closing her notebook and placing it aside, her mind shifted from the weighty matters of her investigations to the simple joy of spending time with her family.

With a happy smile, she rose from her desk, leaving behind the clutter of paperwork, and joined her husband and their daughter Sarah, who was bundled up snugly in her warmest winter coat.

A flashback... Another Sarah... Coughing in a tent... The rain pelting the tarpaulin roof.

Stop.

Henryk's gaze fixed her. Nothing escaped those azure blue eyes. He was at her side in two steps.

"There's no need, darling. We are here. This Sarah. This

Henryk." His voice with its beloved Polish lilt snapped Anna out of her flashback. Strong arms went around her, their little daughter happily gurgling in between her parents.

"Park, park!"

"I'm sorry," Anna murmured, leaning into her small family's embrace. "I was dealing with the war again this morning. Must have triggered the memory. You always see it straight away, don't you, Henryk?"

Henryk kissed her ever so gently. "I do, my darling. You had that exact facial expression the first time we met on Breslau Airport in November 1938. I'll never forget seeing so much pain, so much despair. It humbled me to the bone. I vowed then, as I do now, to do everything in my power to heal your aching heart."

"Oh, Henryk," Anna's glasses misted up as tears welled. "You have healed my heart, repeatedly, even after I broke yours. But let us leave the past for now and take Sarah to see her first snow."

"Snow," the one-year-old cheered. The blue eyes, so much like her father's, sparkled with delight. Dark curls peeked out from underneath her bonnet, a clear Grysnzpan feature.

As they closed the iron gate to their apartment block and stepped out into the crisp January air, the world transformed into a winter wonderland. Battersea Park was blanketed in pristine, white snow, every tree branch adorned with glistening icicles reflecting in the glow of the early afternoon sun.

The air carried the scent of wood smoke from nearby chimneys, mingling with the crisp, clean, winter air that purified the lungs.

Sarah toddled in between her parents, holding tightly onto their hands.

"Snow," she kept repeating taking in the magical transformation of her world, her cheeks flushed with excitement. Anna felt the cold nip at her nose and ears but holding Sarah's little mittened paw in her hand and seeing her daughter's joy, she pushed aside her dislike of cold weather.

"Aren't you freezing?" She gazed sideways at Henryk, who wore no hat nor gloves, his blonde mane blowing in the wind.

"Never!" he quipped. "Ever since flying my Lublin in all weathers and feeling real arctic temperatures in the cockpit, this kind of weather is children's play to me." But Anna saw a shadow gliding over her husband's proud and handsome face, and she remembered how he had told her about having to work in the brickwork section at Sachsenhausen in all weather until every limb was frostbitten.

The war... always that bloody war!

Neither parent wanted to ruin Sarah's outing, so they focused on her, now and then sharing a glance at each other to acknowledge "I'm with you."

Henryk handed Sarah off to Anna to free his hand to scoop up some snow and form it into a ball.

"Look, Sarah." He threw the snowball on the frozen pond where it disappeared in the thick layer of snow that had formed on the surface. "That's what you can do with snow. Make balls. Do you want to make a snowman?"

"Snow!" Sarah cheered, also attempting to scoop up snow and squeeze it between her mittens.

Anna watched with a tender smile how Sarah shrieked with laughter as she threw her snowball just like her father. Her breath formed tiny puffs of condensation in the frosty air.

Together they showed Sarah how to roll a snowball until it got bigger and bigger. Half an hour later Battersea Park had the biggest January snowman, complete with coal for eyes and a carrot as a nose, which Henryk had fetched from the house. Sarah stuck a fallen branch in the snow man's arm to resemble a broomstick.

Anna snapped pictures of Henryk and Sarah, as he held her

high up in the air so she could put an old hat on top of the snow-man's head. Sarah's laughter echoed in the cold air, and she stared up to the sky in wonder when the snow began to fall again.

Soon she was trying to catch snowflakes between her hands. The crunch of her little boots in the snow, while a soft breeze whispered through the trees provided a soothing backdrop to her playful adventure.

In that moment, surrounded by the beauty of the winter land-scape and the warmth of their family bond, Anna vowed to cherish these precious moments forever.

"What's up, my love?" Henryk came to stand next to her and put his arm around her waist. "You seem pensive."

"Did you hear I was with Sable on the phone earlier today? We both got an invitation for an anniversary at our former finishing school in Switzerland. You know the one I went to after Mutti died?"

"Heavens, that certainly is a message from the distant past," Henryk observed. "Are you thinking of going? When's the event?"

Anna shrugged, wiping some snowflakes from her glasses. "Maybe. It's in June. But I can't leave you and Sarah for a couple of days to go to Switzerland."

"Of course you can. If you want to go, you go, Anna Adams Pilecki."

She smiled. Henryk was always so self-assured, so unflappable.

"I'll think about it. Sable said she'd ask Esther whether she got the invitation as well."

"You could contact Esther yourself, can't you? I remember you said you liked her and that you traveled together after war was declared, when Hitler invaded my country." Henryk drew her closer.

"True."

Anna remembered how she'd given Esther a copy of her favorite book at the time, "Rebecca" by Daphne du Maurier.

. . .

"And the ashes blew toward us with the salt wind from the sea."

Anna shivered, reclining further against Henryk's broad chest.

Sarah stuck out her little red tongue, caught a white snowflake and swallowed it. "Yum."

PART II

THE REUNION

SWITZERLAND JUNE 1948

10

AGNÈS AND MADELEINE

Paris, 15 June 1948

A gnès and Alan's city garden, nestled in the heart of Neuilly-sur-Seine, was a hidden oasis of tranquility, a lush sanctuary amidst the hustle and bustle of urban life.

Though not expansive in size, every inch of space was meticulously cared for, a testament to the mistress of the house's passion for gardening and her green thumb.

A winding stone path meandered through the garden, flanked by trimmed boxwood hedges that formed natural boundaries and created an intimate and secluded atmosphere.

Bright bursts of color punctuated the borders, as vibrant blue delphiniums fought for space with cheerful yellow coreopsis, and globe amaranths from purple to white stood proudly in the middle.

Agnès, herself usually modestly dressed in toned-down blues and greens, loved blooms spilling over in flower beds, painting a scene Vincent van Gogh would have approved of, in hues of crimson, violet, and gold.

Slender-stemmed Bay trees with a full crop of leaves provided the necessary shade, casting a playful pattern of shadows on the ground below.

A charming, stone fountain served as the centerpiece of the garden, fat stone carp spouting water that sparkled in the sunlight and provided a soothing clatter of background melody.

Ivy climbed the walls of the surrounding buildings, softening the edges with its verdant tendrils and adding a touch of wild beauty to the urban setting.

A wrought iron bench stood beneath a canopy of climbing roses, inviting visitors to pause and take in the sights and sounds of Agnès's enchanting Eden.

At the end of the garden, a green and white painted garden house, with glass French doors, served as a hideout against both rain and shine.

The June sun bathed the garden in a warm embrace, while the scent of freshly cut grass mingled with the fragrant aroma of blooming flowers.

In the shade of the garden house, Agnès and Madeleine sat comfortably against the cushions of their wicker chairs, sipping afternoon tea from delicate porcelain cups.

From the garden next door, the tinkling laughter of children playing added to the idyllic ambiance, reminding them of the joys of motherhood.

"I simply can't believe the loveliness of your garden, *ma chère*, you certainly are *une jardinière extraordinaire*! Those hands of yours cannot just heal people, but also tend plants like no other. *Vous êtes une guérisseusse universelle*," Madeleine marveled, followed by her clear laughter sounding not unlike that of the neighbour's children. "*Oh pardonnez-moi.* Listen to me. I put one foot on French soil and ta-da-da the English language totally escapes me."

Agnès laughed with her friend. "I'm not sure I'm a universal healer, Maddy, but I'd sure like to be that. And never mind speaking French. You seem to forget I'm French too. I've only taken to speaking English since being around Alan. If you prefer to speak French, *faites comme bon vous semble!* Be my guest."

"*Non, non, non!*" Madeleine voiced. "You are expecting an international entourage. Let's prepare for that. Though all but you underwent Madame Paul's Swiss French, many of of the girls aren't native French speakers."

"It's quite something, isn't it?" Agnès mused. "I had never expected to host six Resistance women under my roof. And they're all friends, despite coming from all over Europe."

"You're forgetting the two veterans, Aggie. You and I were resistance women *avant la lettre* during the First World War." Madeleine wagged a tapered finger with perfect coral nail varnish.

As the sun sunk lower and dipped under the roof of the garden house, she took her cat-eye sunglasses from her bag. As she put them on, she became the spitting-image of Rita Hayworth, the same thick, wavy auburn hair, the curved eyebrows, the perfect shape of her classical-beauty, full, glossy lips.

"How can I ever forget us, Maddy? Those were the days...we were young and innocent. Though I'd do it all over again, if I could."

"Me too," Madeleine said in a dreamy voice. "And I don't see *ma soeur* Elle *et mon frère* brother Jacques often enough. Did you know Jacques's daughter Daphne was with *La Résistance*, just like Océane? My little niece helped liberate Paris. Then she went on to marry a Congolese merchant called Paul Bâh. They fought together in the war, but both adore fashion, so they launched a couture house, DragonBâh Chic. Gorgeous clothes. I ordered a *une robe d'été*, a summer dress from them that I'll wear to the party at Le Manoir."

Agnès nodded. "Yes, I heard about that success story from Océane. Isn't it fantastic? Maybe we could all visit the couture house when we come back from Switzerland? I'd love to meet Daphne and her husband."

"Oh, that would be *magnifique!*" Madeleine's eyes sparkled, "Daphne is such a doll. She keeps telling me I was her big example in World War I, you know running away from Le Manoir and fleeing to Château de Dragoncourt. I was hardly a good example of *une tante.*"

"You were cute, whatever you did, Maddy. And that monkey of yours, LouLou was sweet too."

Madeleine's eyes darkened, "Ah, *ma Louloute.* I miss her so. Daphne has a pet macaw called Liberté. She went missing from Dragoncourt in the war but thankfully she found her way back."

"And how are Jacques and Elle?" Agnès asked. "I haven't spoken with them for ages. We need to get together some day and talk about our time when Château de Dragoncourt was a temporary hospital. I'm sure our husbands would love that too."

"Excellent idea. Gerald would be all for it. And then we should also invite those nurses. What were their names again?"

"The Scottish one was called Bridget, I think, and then there was a nurse called M-C, Agnès recalled.

"That's it! Marie-Christine." Madeleine clapped her hands. "Such a solemn and silent little bird, but nerves of steel. Do you also remember that quaint Eton friend of Jacques'? He did all sorts of odd jobs and was totally in love with Elle, writing her poetry every day."

"Philip Lane, the Earl of Timberwood and Pottery," Agnès and Madeleine cheered at the same time.

"You ladies seem to be having a great time. Mind if I join?" Alan's tall frame leaned against the doorpost.

"Alan! My absolute favorite doctor in the whole world. We were just talking about you!" Madeleine rose and kissed him three times on his clean-shaven cheeks. Though she was a tall woman herself, she had to stand on her toes to reach him.

"Speak of the devil? That kind of stuff?" Alan joked back. "Ah Madeleine, my absolute favorite countess in the whole world." Alan bent to kiss his wife.

"You are early, darling," Agnès smiled, feeling the teapot with two hands. "Let me go and get you some fresh tea."

"Thankfully it wasn't busy at the hospital and Doctor Barnard kindly offered to supervise the rest of the shift on her own. Just pray she doesn't need to page me in the next hour. Thinking I'd be more useful around here, I sped home, but I see the gang hasn't arrived yet?"

Alan took the teapot from his wife's hands. "You sit here and chat with Madeleine. It's not like you get a chance to see each other every day. Wouldn't you rather have champagne than more tea? Got some excellent Veuve Cliquot in the fridge."

Agnès and Madeleine looked at each other and nodded. "Small glass for me, darling, you know, I'm not good with alcohol," Agnès called after her husband, who was already disappearing along the garden path.

"So what time are you expecting 'the gang,' as Alan calls them?" Madeleine settled back in her chair and crossed one slender leg in her pressed white pants over the other.

"Let me see," Agnès counted on her fingers. "Sable, Esther, Anna, and Edda are about to arrive at Gare du Nord. Lili's with Océane and the babies, so they will get here when they get here. I guess they have as much to catch up on as we do."

"Oh, I can't wait to see your grandsons! She will bring them, won't she?" Madeleine called out.

"Of course! Océane will wait until Bertrand and Max wake from their afternoon nap. You know they live around the corner from here."

"Grandchildren are such a blessing," Madeleine mused. "I love looking after little Zack when Lili's at the Colliery. I live for those days."

"Couldn't agree more," Agnès smiled.

"*Champagne pour mesdames!*" Alan appeared again, balancing a silver tray with two tall flutes with sparkling liquid. The afternoon sun made the bubbles dance. "I've added something for you to nibble on."

"I thought you were joining us, Alan?" Agnès asked in a surprised voice.

"I was, but Arthur and Daniel feel positively left out with all the resistance girl bustle going on, so I've promised to take them to the station to collect the girls. Giving Jean-Jacques a hand."

"Has he arrived with the minivan?" Agnès rose to go and greet her son-in-law.

"He has, but no, you sit down and enjoy your bubbles, my dear. JJ and I have it all under control. We may not be resistance girls, but men, too, have a flair for organisation, clandestine or not," Alan quipped and disappeared again while Agnès and Madeleine laughed out loud.

"I can hardly believe it's going to happen," Madeleine reflected, her amber eyes sparkling with anticipation. "We've never even met all the girls and now this reunion. Whatever we may think of Madame Paul, she made this happen."

"She did. Honestly, I can't wait to meet the illustrious lady," Agnès observed, "I have no clue what to expect but I'm looking forward to it."

"Don't set your expectations too high," Madeleine snickered, "but I'm secretly with you. Can't wait for this expedition to become a reality and lay my eyes on the Sphinx once more."

The gentle afternoon breeze carried the faint scent of lilacs, causing Agnès to close her eyes and inhale deeply. "I'm sure the girls will be thrilled to see each other again, to reminisce about all our adventures and share stories of how life has changed since the war."

Madeleine nodded in agreement, a fond smile gracing her lips as she sipped her champagne. "And to think our daughters and their friends will have the chance to witness first-hand the strength and resilience of the women who came before them. It's a legacy worth celebrating."

As they continued to chat, the distant sound of a car stopping in front of the house caught their attention. Agnès glanced up. "They're here! Let's go and greet them, Maddy!"

Arm-in-arm they left the garden through the garden gate. Agnès's heart swelled with excitement as she spotted Jean-Jacques opening the side door of the van, a broad grin on his face.

Arthur was bouncing up and down in his wheelchair on the pavement, while Daniel peered into the van as if it held some rare and exotic species. Alan was unloading suitcases from the trunk.

As the two World War I heroines made their way towards the waiting group, laughter and chatter from within the van filled the air, blending seamlessly with the buzz of the long-since liberated City of Light.

And in that moment, surrounded by the warmth of friendship and the promise of adventure, Agnès and Madeleine knew the imprint they'd left on this next generation was one of harmony and friendship as they all embarked on this journey *together*.

11

COMING TOGETHER

A few hours later

Around the Bells' beautifully set dinner table, the group of six junior resistance girls and two senior ones, sat in a mix of anticipation and reunion joy. The men in their midst listening in to the women's chatter with great interest.

Outside beyond the open French doors, the balmy June evening cast a golden glow over the city, bathing the dining room in a warm, inviting light until the sun slowly sank beyond the buildings.

The electric lights were switched on and the doors closed against the mosquitos.

Plates of exquisite French cuisine adorned the table, each dish a testament to the culinary mastery of the Bells' loyal housekeeper and chef, Madame Claudette.

She had hired two maids to serve the Savory coq au vin and delicate ratatouille that tantalized the senses, while glasses of fine Bordeaux wine added a touch of sophistication to the meal.

Edda from Holland, her graceful posture indicative of her career as a ballerina, sat beside Esther, the Norwegian commando fighter, their bond evident in the subtle nods and knowing glances they exchanged.

Sable, the Scottish ambassador, occupied a seat next to Anna, the former spymistress, their eyes darting around the room as if still taking in their surroundings with the keen awareness of seasoned operatives.

As they settled into their seats, the atmosphere was tinged with a hint of hesitation, the air filled with the weight of unspoken memories and shared experiences.

The three sworn friends, Océane, Lili, and Esther, immediately gravitated towards each other, their laughter and animated chatter filling the room as they eagerly caught up on lost time.

Meanwhile, Sable, Anna, and Edda observed the scene in a more reserved demeanor, their expressions betraying a mixture of curiosity and apprehension in this unknown setting.

Agnès and Madeleine, ever the gracious hostesses, made a concerted effort to involve them in the conversation, drawing them into the lively discourse with tales of past adventures and shared triumphs.

Until, Agnès tapped her crystal glass with a knife and the lively chatter gradually subsided. All eyes turned to her, the eldest of the resistance girls and gracious hostess of the evening.

Standing regally at the head of the table, the baroness cleared her throat and began to speak, her voice resonating with a quiet strength that commanded attention.

"My dear friends and family,"

she began, her gaze sweeping over the gathered group with a mixture of warmth and solemnity. She let her blue eyes rest for a moment on her sons, her husband and son-in-law, conscious of their uncommon position in this female ensemble.

"Tonight, as we gather around this table, I am reminded of the extraordinary journey that has brought us together once again."

As her eyes were alight with the memories of a bygone era, she continued,

"we have weathered the storms of war, two wars, faced unimaginable challenges, and stood shoulder to shoulder in the face of adversity. And yet, through it all, we survived. We were the lucky ones. Let us not forget that."

She turned to Madeleine, a fond smile playing at the corners of her lips.

"Dear Maddy, we used to call you Mad-Maddy, and dear Alan, how far we have come since those dark days of what we used to call the Great War. From the trenches of World War I to the clandestine operations of World War II, we have shared a lifetime of trials and triumphs."

Agnès's gaze then shifted to the younger generation, her heart swelling with pride but also with concern.

"And now, as we embark on this journey to reunite with Madame Paul at Le Manoir, and relive the memories of your youth, I am keenly aware that only Océane and Lili are still blessed with both living parents. And Anna still has her father. The other girls, Esther, Sable, Edda and my son Daniel must do without your elders and your children will have to do without their grandparents. Know that

we share in your grief and honor the legacy of those who came
before us and carry their spirit with us into the future."

It was typical of Agnés's great heart that she could and would
mention the big pain point that most of the girls shared.

Faces fell, hands were squeezed under the table, but then they
all saw Esther rise from her chair, tall and blonde and with that
quiet intensity burning in her light green eyes. Eyes that had seen
into the depths of pain. She made a graceful bow to Agnès and Alan.

"Dear friends and kind hosts,"

she began, her clear voice carrying a somber yet resolute tone as
she addressed them.

"After Madame Bell spoke so eloquently, I feel a need to say
something on behalf of the younger generation. As we gather here
tonight, I am all too aware of the weight of our shared history and
the profound losses that have shaped each of our lives."

Her words resonated with the heavy memories of loved ones
lost.

"Though I want to keep it light, it is true that for some of us, the
scars of war run deep, cutting through generations and leaving
behind gaping wounds that may never fully heal."

She paused, allowing her gaze to dart to young Daniel who sat
very straight and very still, clearly in awe of this imposing Nordic
fighter with her great composure. A moment of silence settled over
the room, a tangible acknowledgment of how each of them had
suffered in the past war they had all endured.

"I stand before you as a witness to the atrocities of the Holocaust, having lost both my parents, my young brother, my aunt and my fiancé to its unfathomable cruelty,"

Esther's voice lost its steadfastness only slightly, betraying some of the rawness of her emotions.

"But, I am also acutely aware that the spectre of death and loss has haunted each of us in its own way. Whether it be through illness, collaboration, or the brutality of the Gestapo, we have all borne witness to the indiscriminate ravages of war."

Though her words were hard to bear, they all felt what Esther voiced needed to be said to reach the next level of healing - healing together, healing as a group.

She turned to Agnès and Alan, her expression softening with gratitude.

"And yet, with our wounds in the past, our future looks much brighter for each of us and here we are. Thank you for having opened your home to us with unwavering hospitality and generosity. We are so grateful to be able to share this moment together. Alive."

Esther's eyes shimmered with unshed tears as she raised her glass in a solemn toast.

"To Agnès and Alan, our steadfast friends, and gracious hosts. May your kindness and compassion serve as a beacon of light after the darkness that lies behind us, guiding us away from the trials we faced. Each in our own way."

As the room echoed with the gentle clink of crystal and the

murmur of agreement, Esther's words hung in the air like a solemn vow, a testament to the resilience of the human spirit and the enduring power of friendship in the face of adversity.

As they prepared to embark on their journey the next day, they now knew they did so with hearts heavy from loss yet buoyed by the strength of their shared bonds and the promise of a brighter tomorrow.

"Hear! Hear! The words of a true leader!" Sable clapped her hands, her blue eyes brimming over with tears. Most around the table were retrieving handkerchiefs, blowing noses, and dabbing eyes.

"Oh, Esther, you'd never have spoken up like this during our Manoir days but listen to you now. You deserve all the happiness that comes your way, my dear friend." Océane uttered, clamping Bertrand against her chest, while Jean-Jacques cradled Max.

Edda just placed her hand, gracefully on Esther's arm. "Thank you for including my pain about my parents, which – thank God – is a minority. But I had my share. And I will forever be glad Asher was with Carl in his last moments. Their bond will never die, whatever the Nazis tried."

"Thank you, Edda, I agree. It gives me some peace of mind too knowing the two sworn friends were together." Esther sat down again. Her eyes darted to Anna across from her.

"And dear Anna, you don't know how much comfort Daphne du Maurier's *Rebecca* gave me during those long years of the war. I think I could recite the whole book if needed. It was my anchor in a wild, wild sea."

Anna pushed up her glasses. Her dark eyes were moist. She'd been silent so far, overtaken by emotions. She'd had to stay so strong, so on top of everything for years that she still wasn't able to relax and feel the depth of her losses.

But revisiting these familiar people from the past, hit her with a wave of both pain and understanding. She too, had survived the worst of it.

"I'm glad to hear it," she said in a small voice. "The same book gave me much comfort during some of *my* dark days. It's strange, isn't it, how a poem or a story can lift us up and give us hope?"

"I love reading," Daniel chimed in, clearly beaming at being able to contribute his bit. "It's comic strips for me, like Superman and Captain Marvel."

"I love Bugs Bunny and Wonder Woman. And now you all sit and be merry!" Lili commanded in her very British voice. This broke the rather subdued spell and as the sweet aroma of chocolate soufflé wafted through the air, the conversation took on a lighter tone.

Whilst the evening progressed, the barriers between old friends and new acquaintances began to melt away, replaced by a sense of camaraderie and shared purpose.

Even Arthur and Daniel ventured to interject a random remark and take part in the playful banter, adding a youthful energy to the gathering.

Amidst the laughter and conversation, there was an undercurrent of excitement and anticipation, for in the morning they would embark on a journey that reunited them with Madame Paul, the enigmatic schoolmistress of Le Manoir, whom none of the participants apparently had really understood.

Mixed feelings about the reunion still swirled in the air, complex emotions that accompanied the prospect of revisiting old haunts and confronting past demons.

Océane leaned over to Lili, excitement gleaming in her eyes. "Can you believe we're actually doing this? I mean, Es and you and I swore two years ago in *À La Petit Chaise* on the Rue de Grenelle we'd hate Madame Paul 'til our dying days."

Lili nodded with a laugh, her red curls bouncing with each movement. "I know! And here we are. Facing the Sphinx head on. I wonder if we'll slip back into mischief and fear of being found out as soon as we set foot on the gravel courtyard."

Then her smile disappeared, "I'm so going to miss the chauffeur and my dear brother in arms, Filippo Maltese. But no thinking of him now. I said I would be merry."

From next to them Esther chipped in, "Ah, yes, those were the days! Fear of being found out." Her eye sought out Sable, who'd clearly followed their conversation.

"I sincerely wish I could turn back the time and never set you up in the music room as I did, Esther dear. You know that. I'm so glad we've been able to step over our shadows during our commando training days in Shetland."

Ever the diplomat, Sable placed a hand over her modest bosom. "Never again will I partake in betraying our sisterhood. If the war has taught me one thing, it's that us women must stick together and always have each other's backs."

"So, no sneaking out for a smoke or explore the streets of Lausanne under cover of night for you, Sable?" Anna inquired, smirking.

"Are you tempting me, Anna dear? For I'll as easily knot some sheets together to escape or slide down the drainpipe. It will be an elementary exercise after the SOE trainings we've had."

In her turn, Sable raised her glass in a toast. "To old friends and new beginnings. May our reunion be filled with laughter, love, and perhaps a hint of danger."

Edda, usually on the more serious side like Anna, smirked, a mischievous glint in her dark eyes. "Now I haven't got a broken foot, I'm sure I can join in and finally get into some trouble too, especially if these two joined as well."

She gestured towards the two teenage boys, who were busy engaged in a heated debate over the latest football match.

"Oh Mom, can we come too?" Arthur instantly chirped.

Agnès smiled warmly, "Another time, son. This one is ladies-only."

"*Ah non, ce n'est pas juste*! How unfair," both boys observed at the same time, but soon returned to their own conversation.

Madeleine, who'd followed the entire conversation with a fine smile on her ladylike face, hadn't spoken so far but now said in a voice tinged with a hint of nostalgia. "Here's to us, the Resistance Girls, united once again to celebrate the bonds of friendship that have stood the test of time."

As they raised their glasses for the final time, the clink of crystal resonated throughout the room, a poignant reminder of the strength and resilience of women in wartime and beyond.

They continued to share laughter and stories late into the night, the promise of the upcoming adventure hanging in the air like a beacon guiding them towards a future filled with possibility and promise.

12

THE JOURNEY

The next day - Paris, 16 June 1948

I n the early morning, as the first rays of sunlight streamed through the bay windows of Agnès and Alan's Parisian home, the girls gathered around the breakfast table, cups of steaming coffee and plates of fresh croissants before them.

With the anticipation of their journey to Switzerland looming, Océane turned the conversation to the topic of a hostess or anniversary gift for Madame Paul.

"Golly," Sable exclaimed, "what a goose I am. I totally forgot how impolite it would be to arrive empty-handed. Thank you for your French consideration, OC."

Unperturbed Océane suggested, "I was thinking we could bring her a selection of French chocolates. They're such a classic gift, and who doesn't love chocolate?"

"They might melt in the car," practical Anna joined in.

Edda looked sceptical as well, "Aren't the Swiss a bit snobby about having the best chocolate in the world?"

"We have Valrhona, Monnat, Menier. As if they can't compete with Lindt and Callier! And Jean-Jacques is going to fill some boxes with ice for our lemonade, so we could store the chocolate in there," Océane protested.

Lili nodded in agreement, her freckled nose wrinkling in mischief. "I think gifting her chocolate would demonstrate we at least wish Madame Paul nothing but sweetness."

They all laughed.

"Alright, but do we have time to go out and buy chocolate?" Esther added. "I was thinking maybe we could also get her a beautiful journal or a set of stationery. Something she can use to record her thoughts and memories."

"She'll have plenty to remember us by after our whirlwind visit," Sable snorted, "but I'm not sure she'll want to record those memories!"

Edda interjected, her Dutch accent adding a touch of charm to her words. "Both chocolate and stationery are wonderful ideas, but what about flowers? A bouquet of fresh flowers would bring a touch of beauty and elegance to Le Manoir. Things Madame Paul appreciates."

Esther listened to the various suggestions, her light brow furrowed in contemplation as she took a sip of her coffee. "I think all of these ideas have merit," she said finally, "but perhaps instead of choosing just one gift, we could each contribute some money and buy her a selection of gifts. That way, we can show our appreciation for her in a variety of ways."

The other girls nodded in agreement, the idea resonating with them. "And we can buy the bouquet once we arrive in Switzerland," Sable suggested, "that way the flowers won't be wilting before we even present them to her and get that look of hers."

Sable acted as if putting her glasses on that were hanging from two pearls strings on her bosom and looked around the table with a piercing and reprimanding look. Hilarity raised up so loudly, Arthur and Daniel stuck their heads around the breakfast room door.

"What are you doing?" Arthur demanded.

"We're writing a play we will perform for our former headmistress," Lili joked.

"Can we watch?" Daniel asked.

"Alas," Lili raised her hands in a gesture of regret, "we've just finished the dress rehearsal and now have to pack."

The boys disappeared again. With the decision about the gifts for Madame Paul finalised, the girls set about pooling their resources, each contributing their share towards the collective gift.

"The mothers will chip in as well," Océane put forth, counting the stack of francs, "so we can buy her some decent presents."

As the Citroën Type H, with Jean-Jacques at the wheel, made its way through the streets of Paris, the girls rolled down the windows to feel the wind in their hair and take in the last of the Paris scenes.

With Max and Bertrand tucked away safely in their travel cot at Océane's feet, the infant twins were shaded from sun and wind.

From nearby cafés the scent of freshly baked bread wafted their way, mingling with the aroma of coffee. A fragrance that tantalized their senses.

The temperature outside was warm but comfortable, the gentle breeze carrying with it the promise of a beautiful summer day.

With all faces turned to the open windows, the sights of Paris unfolded like a vibrant tapestry, the iconic landmarks of the city – the Eiffel Tower, the Arc de Triomphe, the Sacre Coeur, and the bustling boulevards lined with charming bistros and boutiques – passed by in a blur of color and motion.

Inside the van, the atmosphere was alive with the sound of

laughter and chatter, the joyful banter of old friends reunited after too long apart.

As they drove farther away from the heart of the city, the scenery began to change, giving way to tree-lined streets and quaint villages nestled against the backdrop of rolling hills.

Now the scent of freshly cut grass and wildflowers filled the air, and the earthy aroma of the countryside.

The chatter of the eight resistance girls never died, their voices mingling with the drone of the engine and Jean-Jacques whistling La Marseillaise.

The atmosphere was one of high anticipation, reminiscent of a school outing, complete with the occasional high-pitched shriek of laughter and low fives slapping each other's hands.

"So, who's ready for some Turkish Delight? I bought them when we purchased Madame Paul's chocolate. They're very sticky, but so yum-yum." Sable exclaimed, her eyes sparkling with excitement as she passed around a box of colored cubes sprinkled with powdered sugar.

"What is Turkish Delight?" Edda asked, gazing down at the assortment in surprise.

"Oh, not for you," Sable joked. "It's pure sugar, like candied fruit. It'll ruin your ballerina waistline."

"Then I'll have two," Edda quipped and put both in her mouth, her cheeks bulging out like a frog's.

Laughter erupted from the group as they eagerly reached for the sweets.

"Those Turks know what girls like us want," Anna smirked, losing her former seriousness as she rolled her eyes behind the thick glasses.

"I don't even know if the Turks have anything to do with this delight," Sable observed, "but we'll give them credit for our moment of peak delight."

As the van rumbled along the winding roads, a soft whimper broke the cheerful chatter. Bertrand, the younger of the four-week-old twins, stirred in his cot, his tiny face contorted in a silent cry.

Edda, herself mother to eight-month-old daughter Addey, immediately leaned over to offer her support. "It's okay, little one," she cooed, gently rocking the travel cot. Océane was already tugging on her clothes, ready to feed his hungry little mouth.

As Bertrand contently sucked his mother's breast, the topic of babies was now on everyone's minds. Photographs were handed around of Zack with Lili and Iain and with grandparents Madeleine and Gerald.

Edda proudly showed the sweet little face of her Addey and everyone gasped at her curls and lovely round face.

"What about you, Sable? How old is Isabella now?" Agnès inquired. Sable was already searching her purse and brought out a picture of a self-confident girl looking straight into the camera with a smile copied from Shirley Temple. Apart from the blond plaits, her facial expression was exact copy of her mother.

"Our little handful is now eleven, but if you told me she was fourteen I would believe you," Sable sighed. "Oh and her latest caprice is she wants to be called Bella. Now that we live in Paris, she thinks it sounds more French."

"She's adorable. What a strong face," Madeleine admired, "strong mothers get strong daughters, Sable. You'd better prepare for a strong Addey too, Edda." Madeleine pinched Lili's arm in a friendly way and Agnès, though sweet-charactered like Océane, shared a knowing smile with her daughter as well.

Anna had kept quiet but was now bombarded with questions about her young daughter.

"How old is Sarah now? Who is Sarah named after? Do you have a picture? Show us, show us."

"Alright! Alright!" Anna staved them off. "Sarah's eighteen

months now, and yes she's named after one of the sisters I lost, and yes I have a picture."

"She's a bonnie child!" Sable announced, having had the honor of meeting the little Adams-Pilecki sprout. The photograph of the girl with dark curly hair and striking blue eyes looked straight them.

"Is she really only eighteen months? She looks very wise for her age," Agnès remarked.

"Oh, she is a clever one." Anna rolled her eyes. All the while Esther had kept quiet but couldn't hold back any longer.

"Actually, I have some news," she announced, her voice hardly under control from the excitement. "I'm nearly six months pregnant."

Gasps of surprise echoed through the van as the other girls turned to look at Esther, their eyes wide with astonishment.

"Congratulations! That's fantastic! How are you feeling?" one exclaimed after the other, reaching out to offer their heartfelt well-wishes and kissing Esther on the cheeks.

"Six months? How is it possible we missed that?" the two doctors aboard exchanged glances of disbelief. "Show your belly," Océane ordered, and Esther flattened her dress over a very modest, growing belly.

"Everything is fine, the baby is growing alright. I just seem to carry him or her rather deep. My doctor says it's my abdominal muscles. As a commando and ski instructor, I've done so much physical exercise, my muscles refuse to give way."

"Oh, my Good God in Heaven!" Lili cried out. "Can you believe it? We have not only all survived that dreck of a war, but we're also all going to have a next generation. If that isn't triumph, I don't know what is."

Esther was immediately put in the best seat, where she had more leg space and the freshest air.

Jean-Jacques, who'd stopped his whistling and was listening

from behind the wheel, chuckled softly. "Looks like I'll have to drive even more carefully with all these new mothers and a mother-to-be on board."

The older two women, observing the scene with fondness, exchanged a knowing glance. "It seems with motherhood in the air, this is really a wonderful get-together," Agnès remarked with a smile.

"Indeed," Madeleine agreed, her eyes twinkling with pride. "To see their happiness is such a beautiful thing to see."

As the Citroën continued its slow trek through the French countryside towards the Swiss border, the bond between the Resistance Girls grew stronger than ever, united by the shared joys and challenges of motherhood and the enduring strength of their friendship.

13

THE ARRIVAL

Fifteen hours later - Le Manoir, , 17 June 1948

As the large van rolled to a stop at the borders of Lake Geneva, the tired travelers stirred from their exhaustion-induced daze. The soft glow of moonlight danced on the tranquil waters of the lake, a play of cold light and deep dark that was both soothing and unsettling.

The Alps on the other side of the inky water were veiled in a dense, nightly mist and the mountain air was crisp, almost frosty. A male tawny owl uttered a wavering hoo-hoo sound to warn its female of the nightly disturbance. She responded with a sharp ke-witt, ke-witt and fluttered away from a nearby spruce.

Sable stirred first. She'd been fast asleep but was instantly on high alert. Her agent instinct kicked in. *Where am I? What do the surroundings look like? Is there an escape route?* Something in her reaction alerted Esther, the other former, active combatant in enemy territory.

"It's only the Sphinx we're facing at Le Manoir, Sable," Esther whispered in the dark. "We can handle her with our little pinkie, if needed."

The joke, and the recognition of her momentary flashback, made Sable smirk and relax.

"Will we ever not be secret agents?" she whispered back.

"In time, I'm sure," Esther replied, "but our training was rigorous and our experiences so intense, it won't wear off easily."

"I know," Sable agreed. "It's taken me a year to get accustomed to not carrying a gun in my pocket."

Esther nodded, "totally there with you."

The rest of the company woke up one by one, yawning and stretching. Madeleine had insisted on driving the last stretch of the journey to give Jean-Jacques some much-needed rest.

She jumped out of the driver's seat, thrusting her arms in the air and stamping her feet against the chill.

Then she stood perfectly still, inhaling the clean, freshwater aroma mingled with the earthly scent of the shoreline. So different from the briny breeze on top of Dover's cliffs.

The Swiss air stirred something deep in her, a memory of decades ago, when she'd come here as a recalcitrant seventeen-year-old, for the first time away from her parents and siblings, homesick and angry.

Madeleine suppressed the old anger that flared up in her now. The anger had been rather silly! Then and now.

But there had been a war raging in her homeland, turning the family's château in Picardy into an emergency hospital for the wounded on the front and she... Madeleine de Dragoncourt, the queen of daredevilry and spunk, had been shipped off to a backwater finishing school in Switzerland far away from all the exciting action.

Isn't it a strange feat? Madeleine thought, taking a deep breath to calm herself, *how scent brings back all those long-forgotten memories.*

"Are you alright, Maman?" Lili had come to stand next to her, wrapping an arm around her mother's slender waist and leaning into her.

"*Ah oui*! I'm fine. And you?" Madeleine gazed at her daughter's frazzled face in the dim light.

"It's strange to be back here. I don't know what I'm supposed to be feeling, but it's a mixture of everything: nostalgia, innocence, resistance," Lili pondered. "I'm glad you're here with me, Maman. And all the girls."

They stood together in the still of the night, until Lili whispered. "Do you hear the rustle of the wind in the leaves? It's heaven after the drone of the car's engine for hours. And smell those pine trees? And hear the lapping of the waves against the shore? It's so good to be out in nature again."

Like her husband Iain, Lili was really an outdoorsy girl who lived for riding Morning Star along the cliffs and hiking through the Scottish Highlands.

"I wonder if Madame Paul is still expecting us?" Agnès wondered, as she joined Madeleine and Lili. The contours of Le Manoir's walls and roofs silhouetted sharply against the black of the night.

Only one light was on, and all eyes turned there. At some point in their finishing school career, they'd all been in that office for reasons not everyone was keen to remember.

"She's awake alright," Sable observed, "probably applying the coral lipstick. Just in case."

The entire group had now gathered, luggage at their feet, secretly glad to be given a moment to collect their thoughts before encountering the austere headmistress.

Taking in deep breaths of air, stretching stiff limbs, yawning, and rubbing sleepy eyes. After all, it was two in the morning.

Finally, the light above the front door flashed on and the double doors to the school's entrance opened wide. Madame Paul came floating down the stairs, straight-backed and picture-perfect in her navy-blue dress, as if time had stood still, with eight pairs of eyes gazing up at her.

"*Bienvenue, mes chéries,*" she greeted them in that voice that still rang familiar in their ears but seemed to have mellowed with time. The hard metallic ring had become softer, sweeter, though sweet was a contradiction in terms when it came to Le Manoir's schoolmistress.

As she took turns shaking that cool, marble hand of her with each, she continued conversing in a tone honed by years of hospitable practice.

"My dears, I know you have arrived past midnight, as originally planned, but I've asked the kitchen to keep a simple supper of sandwiches and tea ready for you before you enjoy a good night's rest. Would that do? Or perhaps a light soup?"

Madeleine who stood closest to Madame Paul took the lead. "Oh, there was no need to go through the bother for us, but it's very kind of you. As a matter of fact, we *are* a tiny bit hungry."

"Certainly, Madame Hamilton. And it was no botheration at all. I can't express how thrilled I am you are all here." She looked around the group of weary travelers, the celestite eyes turning moist, which chilled the bolder ones like Lili and Sable, and made soft-hearted Edda and even Esther and Anna stare down at their shoes.

Madame Paul tiptoed over to Océane and Jean-Jacques who each held onto a handle of the travel cot with their babies in it who were fast asleep. She peeked into the cot and whispered. "Aren't they adorable? But still so tiny. I've made a family room ready for you in my wing with a separate ensuite for the twins. Would you care to go straight to your rooms perhaps? I have ordered supper to be laid out for you there."

She really seemed to have thought of everything. But then hadn't Madame Paul always been an exceptional organizer?

Océane answered with a grateful nod. "That would be very welcome, Madame. We're both exhausted and the babies will need to be fed soon again as well." But turning to her mother, she added. "If that is okay with you, Mom?"

"Sure honey. You make sure you have a good night's rest. I will see you in the morning." Agnès kissed her daughter and son-in-law good night and also bent to kiss her grandsons.

"I've taken the liberty of putting you next-door to the young family, Madame Bell," the headmistress interjected. "I assumed you'd appreciate being close to your family."

"Now come inside, you've been standing in the cold for way too long. I'll ask Jerôme to get the trolley out and to bring all your luggage to your respective rooms, so please don't go exhausting yourselves any further."

With tired but grateful nods, the Resistance Girls followed Madame Paul inside, the heels of their shoes clicking on the stone steps that led to the massive front doors.

As they entered the now well-lit hall, a sense of comfort washed over them, banishing the weariness that had settled in their bones over the past fifteen hours.

The familiar scent of the school enveloped them – a warm, inviting aroma of wood polish and fresh linens. It was a smell that spoke of comfort and hospitality, welcoming them to the timeless beauty of Le Manoir.

What stopped them in their tracks and made them pause, Lili first and foremost, was a large gilded, framed photograph of Filippo Maltese, the Le Manoir's faithful chauffeur. Placed on the small side table, but in a prominent place, the photo was surrounded by a bouquet of fresh flowers, his car keys, and the huge black cap.

A candle flickered, throwing shadows over his very Italian face - the intelligent frank eyes, the black hair, and black moustache.

They all remembered the stocky, talkative chauffeur who'd driven them numerous times to and from the station in the black Renault with the golden lettering.

His kind words for every novice student and his enigmatic wisdom when you got to know him better were unforgettable.

Madame Paul sighed, "*Ah oui,* Monsieur Maltese was such a courageous man for the resistance. And I never knew. I, who thought she knew everything about everyone, I didn't know he was a staunch resistance fighter, and that Mussolini's men were after him."

Lili sniffled as she went to the small remembrance corner and trailed her finger over his portrait.

"You were a dear friend and loyal comrade, Filippo. And you are dearly, dearly missed during this reunion."

Turning away from the memorial table, all eyes took in the entrance hall. Each girl reacted in her own way to the familiar sights and scents of the immense, tiled entrance hall, which was the size of half a soccer field with the broad mahogany staircase leading to the upper floors.

On Esther's face, a mixture of nostalgia and weariness was evident, as she remembered why she first came here, to set up house for her and her fiancé Carl, and how everything had gone wrong. Lili was by her side, not showing much reminiscing, but glad to be in the middle of the group.

Sable put her pointy chin in the air, her nostrils flaring like a horse, ready to enter the battlefield. Anna was by her side, pushing the glasses up the bridge of her nose, adopting that unreadable expression that had carried her and her career as the spymistress through the war.

Edda walked even straighter, a thin smile on her lips as she remembered Bach and walking with five books on top of her head.

Madeleine held onto Agnès's hand, as if finding support in her friend, should Madame Paul decide to shoo her away.

As they gathered around the long table in the dining room, the clinking of cutlery and the murmur of conversation soon filled the air.

The supper was a short affair. Madame Paul kept her words brief, only inviting them to breakfast at nine in the morning, just a few short hours away.

Lili and Esther opted to share a bedroom, while the others chose to have their own, grateful for the opportunity to rest in a place they'd never thought their heads would find a pillow again: Le Manoir.

14

THE SURPRISE

Several hours later

While the morning sun climbed over the Savoyan Alps and twinkled gaily on the surface waters of Lake Geneva, its golden rays spread over the breakfast table at Le Manoir.

The Swiss sun had a special shine, warm and cool at the same time, a brightness only familiar to the mountains.

Some still sleepy, some with spirits buoyed by the promise of a new day, one after the other the Resistance Girls gathered around the table, wearing summer dresses in bright and cheerful colors, hair curled and styled, and cheeks with a dash of powder.

No longer students, some found it hard to know what role to take on in this new situation, but in the presence of the group no one felt left out.

Whatever their mental state, their senses were immediately enveloped by the enticing aromas and mouth-watering sights of a traditional, Swiss breakfast spread.

Freshly baked bread and pastries beckoned from woven baskets, their golden crusts glistening with a hint of the buttery goodness contained within.

Crusty baguettes, soft rolls, and flaky croissants tempted the girls with their fresh-baked aroma, while sweet pastries like pain au chocolat and Swiss-style brioche promised new delights.

Alongside the bread and pastries sat a selection of local cheeses, each one boasting its own unique flavor and texture. Blocks of creamy Emmental, nutty Gruyère, and tangy Appenzeller lay ready to be tasted, alongside slices of air-dried beef and smoked ham, adding a savory element to the breakfast spread.

Pots of homemade jams and preserves adorned the table, their vibrant colors and fruity scents tempting the guests to spread them generously on their bread. From floral raspberry to sweet apricot, each jar offered a burst of flavor that tickled the taste buds.

A large bowl of muesli sat at the center of the table, surrounded by bowls of creamy yogurt and fresh milk. The wholesome combination of rolled oats, nuts, seeds, and dried fruit promised a nutritious start to the day, while the yogurt added a dairy richness to each spoonful.

A platter of fruit completed the breakfast - red apples, ripe pears, and bunches of green and red grapes - adding a touch of freshness to the table.

Coffee and tea were served by two waitresses, who moved as silently and politely around the table as seasoned Le Manoir graduates.

As the Resistance Girls helped themselves to the delicious offerings before them, their senses were overwhelmed by the sights, smells, and tastes of a traditional Swiss breakfast.

And as they savored each bite, they couldn't help but feel grateful for the warm hospitality and comforting familiarity of Le Manoir.

Whatever may have been bad here, the food had never disappointed.

And, for some, seeing all this abundance of food was almost surreal, even three years after the war. Edda, who'd suffered near starvation during the 1944 Dutch hunger winter; the strict rationing that still made cooking a meal in Britain for Madeleine, Lili, and Sable a daily ordeal.

Lili was forever grateful to Iain for producing vegetables from the land and dairy from their goats. But meals in Britain were still a meager affair, certainly compared to the opulence on Madame Paul's table.

The headmistress herself presided over her deluxe table with usual grace and poise. In her signature navy taffeta dress with the invariable glasses on their pearl strings resting on her bosom. Her hair hadn't changed one bit, still ash blonde - possibly dyed after all these years - and stylishly rolled to one side of her slender neck in a French twist.

Not an extra ounce of fat around her waist. Even wrinkles seemed to have been kept at bay by sheer willpower. The same coral lipstick and modest make-up.

Thirty years didn't appear to left a mark on Madame Paul Vierret, at least not on the exterior, perhaps even made her more graceful, more powerful.

Really the only thing that had changed was the softened glance in her eyes. The once-frosty, blue gaze now held a twinkling of unfamiliar care and delight.

As soon as her visitors had satisfied their appetites and corners of mouths were dabbed with pristine white napkins, she looked around the table with something of impatience.

"My dear girls, or rather *mesdames*, I should say," she began, her voice filled with warmth and anticipation, "I have a surprise for you all."

Curious glances were exchanged, interest piqued by what she was about to disclose. They leaned in closer, though no elbow would ever rest on the table when she was near, eager to hear what she had to say.

"In secret," Madame Paul continued, her smile widening, "I have been in contact with Jean-Jacques to concoct a plan."

All eyes turned to Jean-Jacques in utter amazement. *What did he have to do with this?* The confidence man himself pretended to be totally absorbed in spreading apricot jam on a croissant, but Océane who knew him back to front saw he had a hard time suppressing a smirky grin pulling the left corner of his mouth down.

Before she could interrogate her husband, Madame Paul took the lead again.

"To express our gratitude for your courageous contributions to a liberated Europe, your husbands and children will join us today, here at Le Manoir, to join the celebration with us this weekend."

Gasps of surprise and delight filled the room as the realization sunk in.

"But where are they going to stay? I thought this was a girls' only school?" Practical Anna asked.

This evoked a rather un-ladylike wink from the headmistress. "Correct, Madame Pilecki, but don't worry, it's all settled. I've booked the men and the children into the chalet next door, but...," she smiled mischievously, "I am open to any arrangements amongst yourselves. If families want to stay together at Le Manoir and others prefer to go next door to Chalet BelleVue, please feel free to arrange it as befits you best."

They exchanged excited looks, their hearts swelling with happiness at the thought of being reunited with their husbands and children.

Thank you, thank you so much. That is so wonderful. How did you arrange this without us knowing? Everyone was talking over each other.

Anna and pregnant Esther seemed particularly relieved and quite overwhelmed by the gentleness of Madame Paul's invitation. Tears welled up in Edda's eyes, as she thought of her beloved Asher traveling with little Addey all the way from Amsterdam. She couldn't wait to wrap them both in her arms.

Lili's heart skipped a beat at the thought of seeing Iain, but worried whether Sable's precocious Isabella would remain well-behaved.

"I assume the invitation just refers to *les jeunes gens*?" Madeleine asked tactfully, referring to the younger generation.

"*Ah non, non!*" Madame Paul waved a manicured hand. "*Pour vous aussi!* Your husbands and children are equally welcome."

"But how on earth did you do this without me finding out?" Océane demanded. With her no-nonsense cardiologist look she fixed her husband, clearly unwilling to take vagueness for an answer.

He smiled that irresistible, lopsided smile that transported her all the way back to 1938 when she'd first encountered that smile in the Boston Museum of Fine Arts with Eliza by her side and had fallen for the famous French modern artist there and then.

But much had transpired between them in the past ten years and Océane now knew how evasive her husband could be.

"You don't know my every move, my dapper soldier, you know I'm the elusive artis..." he joked.

"Stop it, JJ." Océane gave him a friendly poke between the ribs.

"Okay, okay! Shall I, Madame Paul, or do you want to disclose our secret?"

A youthful blush colored the headmistress's cheeks. "I think they will accept it better from your mouth, Jean-Jacques."

Madame Paul using the artist's first name though she stuck with the formal *vous* almost went by unnoticed, in the anticipation of the reveal of how these two had conspired with one another.

"*Mesdames, alors* my part in this intriguing plot," Jean-Jacques began with a mischievous twinkle in his striking green eyes, his blond hair tousled in an artful disarray.

He cast a quick glance towards Madame Paul, their eyes meeting in a silent exchange of camaraderie and shared secrets, before returning his attention to the breakfast table.

"Get on with it, JJ!" Océane urged him, knowing how he liked being the center of attention. Jean-Jacques Riveau was the exception to the rule among artistic people - he was a full-out extrovert.

"Alright, my love!" He kissed her cheek. "It all started when I stumbled upon Océane's address book in a drawer in our Paris apartment. And no, I wasn't snooping!"

As he spoke, his lopsided smile, that charming quirk of his lips, added an endearing touch to his words, drawing the attention of everyone present.

No one could resist being captivated by the charisma of this great painter and fierce resistance fighter.

"Being the eccentric artist I am," he continued, his voice tinged with amusement, "I couldn't resist the urge to explore its contents. Lo and behold, I discovered a treasure trove of contacts from OC's war years and beyond – addresses of her comrades-in-arms scattered about in London, Inverness, Amsterdam, Oslo, and Deal."

Collective hilarity echoed through the room. Jean-Jacques certainly knew how to tell a tale. Madame Paul's eyes twinkled with mischief and pride as she watched him regale her guests with the report of their covert operation. Though her part in the operation was still unknown.

"OC and I had arranged for us to travel here as a family, and I was aware that all the other *mesdames* had said 'yes' to Madame Paul's invitation. That makes one and one two, right? What's one bloke going to do among all these lofty ladies? Who's going to drink a pint with me and tell some dirty jokes? Soo..." His voice was brimming with glee. "... I contacted Madame Paul, though that made me shake in my boots with fear. *La grande dame de Le Manoir*! Can you imagine? What was she going to say?"

Madame Paul let out a very girlish giggle. "I only applauded his plan. Bravo!" She clapped her hands together, making the girls fall from one surprise in the other. Was this the stern headmistress they remembered, or had the Jean-Jacques charm put a spell on her?

"When I had my supreme blessing and a vow of secrecy," he carried on, "I carefully extracted the necessary information from the address book, ensuring OC remained none the wiser."

"You are terrible!" Océane cried in mock anger.

"Always and everywhere the rebel!" he riposted.

But his words were met with nods of approval and grateful smiles. They all marveled at his ingenuity and bravery. Thanks to Jean-Jacques, the stay at Le Manoir was going to be one grand reunion of families.

How special and how thoughtful. Madame Paul reached out to gently squeeze Jean-Jacques's hand, a silent gesture of gratitude and solidarity.

"And so," he concluded, a twinkle of pride in the green eyes, "with Madame Paul's impeccable planning and a little help from our friends, we managed to organize their arrival today, just in time for the festivities. But I can tell you with certainty, leading a Resistance cell through France was less of an organizational operation than getting gents and babies from all across Europe together at a finishing school on Lake Geneva."

He sat back in his chair mimicking exhaustion as he rubbed the back of his hand over his forehead not without a feeling for the theatrical.

But his lopsided smile lighted up the room as he basked in the joyous reactions of the resistance girls. It was a moment of triumph, a testament to the spirit of love, friendship, and the enduring legacy of their wartime heroism.

"But how are they traveling?" Agnès asked, wondering how they would cope with Arthur's wheelchair.

"They've made the same arrangements you did, so they've gathered in Paris yesterday at your house, Madame Bell. Just after you all left," the headmistress explained. "They rented another large vehicle with ample space for baby carriages and the wheelchair."

"Oh, Alan was in it as well? Now I remember some abruptly-ended phone calls," Agnès said shaking her head. "I thought it funny, as Alan never has secrets from me, but he said people kept phoning the wrong number."

"Yes, my father-in-law was a great help," Jean-Jacques agreed. "And we had some near misses where it almost leaked out."

"I hope you will enjoy this, *mes chèries*, and I can't wait to see your exceptional husbands and the little ones," Madame Paul said warmly.

The room soon filled with the sounds of laughter and chatter, the air alive with the scent of coffee and the fresh bread. Outside, the mountain birds sang sweetly in the trees, their cheerful melodies adding to the sense of joy and anticipation.

When there was a lull in the conversation, Sable ventured to ask, "what happened to you, Madame Paul? I don't want to sound impolite, but you seem... you seem so different from what I remember."

The celestite eyes rested on Sable for a long moment. Everyone was holding their breath now. Would this be the turning point where the Sphinx resurfaced, and Sable was sent to her room? But, no.

"There are no easy words to explain, Madame Brodie, and it is a long story," she finally said in a husky voice. "Most of that story I've worked into the speech I will share tomorrow, but since you're asking..."

She halted, seemed unsure of her words, another novelty when it came to the headmistress whose ready, biting tongue had stung many students.

She shook her head slowly. "No, I will do as I planned. I will give my testimony tomorrow when everyone is present. I just have one favor to ask of you." Again, she waited. The tchup-tchup-tchup of a blackbird sounded from the garden. A distant cow bell rang. The room was silent as a church.

"I would very much appreciate it if you called me Mademoiselle Goldschmidt from now on, or preferably even Miss Elsie if you can manage. I like the English ring to it."

The silence continued. It was a bit awkward. No one dared to say a thing, to ask anything. Until Esther, who sensed more than she knew, slowly rose, went over to the head of the table and said in barely more than a whisper,

"I will call you Elsie if you call me Esther. Let's be done with Madaming and all formality." Esther bowed down and placed a kiss on the headmistress's cheek.

"Esther," Elsie said, her voice thick with tears. She grabbed Esther's hand and pressed it against the cheek that had been kissed. "I've thought of you so often and of you too, Anna. How I wronged you both. And many with you. But no longer, no longer!"

The Resistance Girls turned to see Madame Paul transform into Elsie Goldschmidt before their very eyes, stripping herself of the Monsieur Paul Vierret they'd never known, didn't even know if he existed.

They saw her in a new light, as they sensed the depth of her own ordeal, revealed only in the obviously Jewish name. The formal, French Madame Paul and her sternness and cold demeanor was replaced with kindness and generosity.

In that moment, Le Manoir felt more like home than ever before, a sanctuary where love and friendship could be rebuilt.

15

THE MORNING WALK

I t was a sublime, sunny day in the Swiss Alps. The morning sun shone brightly on the shores of Lake Geneva. The white, triangular sails of pleasure yachts bobbed gaily on the glittering water and the alpine flowers - white edelweiss, purple asters, and violet gentians - bursting into bloom on the mountain slopes.

The cows shook their bells merrily. It was not a day to stay cooped up indoors.

"You go and enjoy the beauty of the morning, girls," Miss Elsie, aka Madame Paul, ordered. "I still have so much preparing to do for our festivities tonight. And the current cohort of students are arriving back from their walking expedition near St Moritz later today."

"I wondered about the quietness in the corridors," Madeleine observed, "it was so different in my days."

"Oh, we're still very much a functioning finishing school," Elsie assured her, "though for how much longer remains to be seen."

There was such a look of relief on her face, they kept quiet, not knowing what was happening but sensing the school mistress was rather elated about a possible, upcoming closure.

"You will also meet some of your former instructors, who have been accompanying the girls on their mountain hike. Monsieur Georges, the art teacher, Monsieur Petrov, the etiquette teacher and, of course, Mademoiselle Brunner, head of housekeeping instructions." The celestite eyes briefly rested on Sable, but with a hint of amusement.

Sable threw her hands in the air in mock protest. "Heavens, I've given up smoking nine months ago, don't tempt me to start again, Elsie."

And she explained how Mademoiselle Brunner had found her smoking in the ironing room where she was supposed to be instructing Esther on how to do the laundry in the Le Manoir way but had no intention of playing the teacher to the meek Austrian put in her care. Esther laughed as well.

"What a goose I was at the time, but wait…" she exclaimed. Then, in a split-second, Esther was by Sable's side and in an even shorter blink had Sable floored and in a tight headlock. Sable screamed with laughter, kicking her legs in the air.

"I didn't know I had this in me at the time." Esther said drily, releasing her friend with a pat on the head. They both sprang to their feet dusting their dresses. Her pregnant belly didn't even seem to be in the way.

"Golly, and that in your condition!" Elsie uttered in surprise. "I must say I pondered self defense lessons lately, but of course nothing like this. It… it doesn't seem to fit the curriculum of a course in high-class etiquette. It's rather unladylike, certainly in a dress, but very impressive nonetheless."

"You shouldn't have challenged me, Esther darling," Sable warned, "but I'll be gentler with you when it's your turn, just in case." And turning to Elsie she added, "It's part and parcel of being a secret agent."

"Out with you, before I stand here gabbing all day." Elsie shooed them outside, and they soon found themselves scrambling downhill to the lake as they'd done so many times during their school days.

They set off on a leisurely walk along the waterside, their voices mingling with the gentle lapping of waves and the soft rustle of leaves in the breeze. The air was filled with the sweet fragrance of wildflowers and pine trees, adding to the idyllic atmosphere of the Swiss countryside.

In pairs, walking arm in arm, their conversation soon turned to the surprising revelations at the breakfast table.

"I still can't believe Tore will travel all the way from Oslo just to be with us here," Esther confided to Sable. "He was worried about me traveling on my own, but he never said a word."

"Neither did Bill," Sable declared. "He's the kind of person who can't keep any secrets, you know, a poetic soul, so I wonder how he did it."

"We'll soon find out," Anna chimed in, overhearing their conversation. "I'm so happy our men will be here."

"And that you can all see my little Addey." Edda beamed at the thought.

"All the children and our wonderful men," Madeleine agreed. "Let's sit down for a while and talk about Elsie. What do you make of her now?"

They sat on the warm stones, taking off socks and shoes to dip their feet in the ice-cold lake water. Screams and giggles followed.

Then they discussed Madame Paul's unexpected decision to change her name to Miss Elsie Goldschmidt and her hints about revealing secrets in her speech the following day.

They wondered aloud about the mysterious past of their former schoolmistress and the reasons behind her changed demeanor.

"Ah well, it's no use hypothesizing," Agnès, the eldest of the band of sisters, put forth. "I'm sure we'll be all the wiser tomorrow night." They all agreed to refrain from further speculations. Whether Madame Paul or Elsie Goldschmidt, some part of the school mistress would always be shrouded in mystery. Only she was the master of what was disclosed and what was kept private.

While chatting, they marveled at the breath-taking scenery, their eyes drawn to the majestic mountains towering in the distance and the shimmering expanse of the lake stretching out before them.

The sound of birdsong filled the air, interspersed with the occasional chirp of a cricket and the distant call of a cuckoo.

Jean-Jacques' ingenious plan to orchestrate a larger surprise reunion was also discussed and admired, which – in its turn – led to sharing anecdotes of their husbands' wartime exploits and their lives after the war. The lead conspirator himself was back at Le Manoir with the twins.

Eight women laughed and reminisced, their hearts light with the joy of reunion and the promise of new beginnings. And as they continued their leisurely stroll along the shores of Lake Geneva, surrounded by the beauty of the Swiss countryside, they felt how a deep healing was taking place through the bonds of friendship and the knowledge that they finally understood each other.

Before the war they had been pursuing lives they never got to realise thanks to the upheaval in the world that derailed even the best of plans.

War had thrown them into the deep, where they had found how strong they really were. And now that enduring spirit of resilience had brought them all together once again.

16

WIVES AND MOTHERS

The next morning - Friday 18 June 1948

As the early morning sun painted the Swiss Alps in hues of gold and rose, the anticipation at Le Manoir rose by the minute.

Late the night before, Elsie had received a phone call that the husbands and children had decided to stay the night over in Geneva as little Sarah and Addey had been too tired to travel the entire distance in good spirits.

So now the Resistance Girls, accompanied by the headmistress and her loyal staff, gathered at the courtyard, their hearts aflutter with excitement, awaited the arrival of the most anticipated cargo of the decade.

"The thrill is almost like waiting for a midnight drop of Allied weapons and ammunition in a German-occupied zone," Sable whispered to Esther.

"This is much better, Sab, as we know it's going to have the desired result," Esther whispered back.

But the anticipated cargo seemed to take forever to arrive, as they hopped from one foot to the other on the neatly raked gravel and peered down the tree-laned road.

Only Océane was at peace, as she had her family already by her side. She inhaled the soft breeze, carrying the scent of wildflowers mingled with the sweet aroma of freshly baked pastries from the kitchen.

The group stood mainly in silence, some arm in arm, but a squeal of delight erupted as they spotted the van slowly making its way up the road towards the school.

First to exit the vehicle was driver Alan. He unfolded his long, lean self from the front seat and stood scanning the group of ladies standing in the morning light.

Dr. Alan Bell was, and always would be, the archetypal surgeon, strong and empathic, skilfully hiding his severe injury courtesy of the German attack in 1918, after which the then very young surgeon Agnès de Saint-Aubin had saved him from paralysis.

Alan's attention was pulled back to the van and he rolled out Arthur's wheelchair, helping his son sit comfortably. Then helping Daniel with his rucksack. Finally, his warm embrace enveloped his wife of thirty years with a sense of homecoming.

"My darling, they insisted we come here to disturb your peace and quiet. I hope you don't mind?" he joked.

"Mom, Maman, you said we couldn't come but here we are!" The boys also threw their arms around their mother. Tears welled up in Agnès's eyes as she was smothered in their embraces.

Madeleine's heart skipped a beat as she caught sight of Gerald, her beloved husband with his ginger mustache and hair, walking the stiff and proud walk of a former army commander.

He approached with their six-year-old daughter Rosalie in tow, who was already wearing her party dress which was now crumpled and soiled with chocolate stains. But her smile was from ear to ear and her blonde curls still held together with an enormous bow.

Despite her immense joy at seeing them, Madeleine tried hard to hide her disappointment that their adopted daughter, Sarah, was not with them.

"Oh, she couldn't come, my dear, but we are here, aren't we?" Gerald's evasiveness only deepened Madeleine's concern that daughter Sarah was left alone in England, but she pushed aside her worries for the moment, focusing instead on the happiness of this reunion.

Lili's heart soared as she caught sight of her dark-haired, farmer-husband Iain with little Zack on his arm. Their son had fallen asleep, and his little auburn tuft of hair was resting against his father's shoulder as he was sucking his thumb. Lili kissed him ever so carefully to not wake him up.

Meanwhile, Océane, already surrounded by her family, took in all the delight around her. She carried Max, while Jean-Jacques had Bertrand cradled in his arms. Their hearts overflowing with love and gratitude for the success of Jean-Jacques's ingenious plan.

Esther just about managed not to cry as she saw her Viking husband, Tore, striding towards her, his presence a comforting reminder of the love they shared despite the trials they had endured.

"Oh *Jeger*, it's so good to see you and little one. I was a bit worried about the two of you," he said as he scanned his wife's face for traces of tiredness and placed his hand on her belly.

"You know I can take care of myself, darling," she laughed, but happily disappeared in his strong arms. Her joy was tinged with sadness as she realized her sister Rebecca was not among the arrivals, but shook the disappointment from her.

The new group was men and children only. Not siblings, no matter how important.

Sable didn't want to admit she was smitten when she caught sight of her Wild Bill. She couldn't suppress her pleasure and grinned widely.

Daughter Isabella threw herself into her mother's arms and wept as if having been sent back to the orphanage again. Their reunion was filled with tender kisses and whispered words of love.

Soon, Isabella's quick eyes sparkled with excitement as she spotted Rosalie, immediately drawn to the theatrical charm of Lili's younger sister. A friendship was born at first sight.

Edda's knees went weak as she embraced Asher and their six-month-old daughter, Addey.

"I'd never thought, I'd never thought," Edda kept repeating. "I'm so grateful you're here."

"Switzerland has been good to me after I was released from the camps, my butterfly girl," Ash whispered in her hair. "I love being back here, where my health was restored. And with you and Addey, it's heavenly."

The elegant dance couple with their little daughter formed a picture of grace and strength unified in beauty.

And finally, Anna's eyes sparkled with joy as she saw her aviator love, Henryk, head for her with Sarah bouncing in his arms, "Mummy, mummy, mummy!"

All smiles lighted up the courtyard as they were reunited at last.

Elsie, still transitioning from her role as Madame Paul, flanked by her team of teachers - Monsieur Petrov, Monsieur Georges, and Mademoiselle Brunner - watched the reunion with tears in her eyes, her heart overflowing with pride and gratitude for the bonds of friendship and love that had brought them all together once again.

As the Resistance Girls and their families embraced and laughed and cried, the courtyard of Le Manoir was filled with the warmth of love and the promise of budding new friendships, also among the men.

Each family walked through the honor guard of students into the school with hearts brimming over with happiness. They knew this reunion was just the beginning of a new chapter in their lives, filled with hope, love, and lifelong bonds.

17

THE SPEECH

Later that evening

As the sun slowly dipped behind the mountain range and evening descended on Le Manoir, everyone gathered in the school theater, dressed in their most festive attire.

Only the smallest ones were asleep in a hastily arranged nursery in the next room, watched over by two student volunteers.

The atmosphere in the theater was charged with anticipation and emotion. The families of the Resistance Girls, along with Le Manoir staff and the current cohort of students, thronged into the elegant space, where the scent of polished wood and old books mingled with the soft sounds of tuning classical instruments drifting from a quartet of musicians sitting in the orchestra pit in front of the stage.

The grand piano sat proudly at the other side of the stage, its black polished surface gleaming in the soft light.

There was no sight of Elsie, but she was expected to arrive any minute, no matter how much she had changed, Elsie would *not* be late.

The theater itself was a grand and opulent space, high ceilings adorned with carved moldings and chandeliers and side lamps casting a warm glow over the room. Rows of plush velvet seats filled the space, their rich burgundy hue adding to the air of sophistication and elegance.

At the front of the room, the stage commanded attention, its velvet curtains the color of the plush seats were drawn closed in anticipation of the evening's events.

As the families settled into their seats, the building emotions of the evening began to stir within them. For Sable, however, the sight of the piano brought forth a tidal wave of memories and emotions she hadn't anticipated.

In a flash, she was back in 1939 the last time she'd been in this room, the night she had set up Esther to play the piano after dinner, breaking Madame Paul's strict rules and unjustly subjecting Esther to punishment.

As the weight of her actions gripped her, Sable felt a lump form in her throat, tears welling up in her eyes as she recalled the hurt she'd caused her now-dear friend. Unable to contain her remorse any longer, she turned to Esther, her voice trembling with emotion.

"I'm so... so... sorry," she stuttered in apology. "I was utterly horrid to you. You, who were only sweet and nice."

"Don't fret, Sab." Esther put a hand on her friend's shaking shoulder. "We've gone over this before. You were hurting and that's why you lashed out. You're long forgiven."

But Sable kept sniffling, accepting Bill's big white handkerchief to blow her nose. The Scotsman looked on in surprise at his otherwise proud and poised wife, but let her settle herself.

The other Resistance Girls, seeing Sable's distress, had no such restraint, and rose from their seats gathering around her in a circle of love and support.

"It was just a childish prank, Sable," Lili told her.

"If we'd known what you had gone through before you came here, we would've helped you instead of cold-shouldered you," Océane reassured her.

"I'm sure you would walk through fire for Esther, if you needed to now," Anna added.

"I love you for your honesty, Sable. You're a really, good person," Edda said lastly.

And so, in the hallowed halls of Le Manoir's theater, surrounded by the echoes of their shared past, they once again stood together, their hearts entwined as they embraced in a group hug.

It was a moment of healing and redemption, a testament to the power of forgiveness and the unbreakable bonds of sisterhood.

A hush fell over the audience as the curtains swung open, revealing an almost empty stage. In the middle stood a comfortable armchair, a microphone on a stand, and a small round table holding a carafe and a single glass.

One single spotlight focused on the scene, the cut crystal of the water glass catching the light. As she stepped onto the stage, all eyes were drawn to the woman before them. Gone was Madame Paul, the austere figure clad in navy taffeta and pearls.

In her place stood Elsie Goldschmidt, a pretty woman in her early sixties, her hair no longer tightly coiffed but instead flowing freely around her shoulders in soft waves that allowed the silver strands to be seen.

The glasses that had once perched upon her nose were nowhere to be seen, allowing her clear blue eyes to shine with newfound warmth and vitality.

Dressed in a simple yet elegant ensemble of flowing fabrics in a lively floral design, Elsie exuded a sense of femininity and easy grace that captivated her audience.

Her posture was still straight but less intense, her movements more fluid and authentic as she moved across the stage towards the armchair with what seemed a newfound sense of freedom and purpose.

She stood perfectly still, facing the audience as she gracefully accepted their standing ovation with an almost diffident smile on her face.

After the applause died down, she seated herself in the armchair, not completely liberated from her schoolmarm habits in the way she neatly arranged the pleated skirt and crossed her legs at the slender ankles.

She drew the microphone towards her, tested it and took a moment to compose herself. There was no sheet of paper in her hand, but all who knew her, knew the words she was going to express had been carefully crafted and rehearsed meticulously.

As she began to speak, her voice rang out with clarity and conviction, carrying the weight of years of wisdom and experience. Gone were the harsh tones and sharp edges of Madame Paul, replaced instead by a gentler, more compassionate presence of Elsie.

"Mesdames et Messieurs, chers invités, anciennes étudiantes, collègues et étudiantes actuelles,
"Tonight, as I am here before you, I am filled with a profound sense of gratitude for the beautiful years I have had the privilege of spending as the schoolmistress of Le Manoir finishing school.

"These halls have been my home, and you, my students, have been my family. In these thirty years, I've watched hundreds of young women like yourselves come through these doors, eager to learn, to grow, and to embark on the journey of womanhood.

"Evidently, I reflected deeply on my decades here while preparing for this anniversary. I was struck by the realization that if it were not for this school, I cannot begin to imagine where I would be today. Le Manoir has been my sanctuary, my refuge from the storms of life, and for that, I am also immensely grateful.

"Yet, I must also acknowledge that in my efforts to portray what I thought were the qualities and characteristics of a finishing school mistress, I may have been too strict and too aloof. Though I regularly consulted with the headmistresses of Brillantmont, Château Mont-Choisi and Mont Fertile, I had to forge my own role and, in my desire to represent the very best finishing school in the region, followed every etiquette and manner to the letter.
"But there was more to it than met the eye."

Elsie stopped speaking and seemed to hesitate while she poured herself some water from the carafe and took a sip. The silence in the room was so poignant one could have heard a star fall from the heavens. Elsie smiled, a real, broad smile.

"I am ready, ready to tell my story and hopefully be forgiven by God and by you, about whom I care the most. Throughout my career I've always kept my personal story at arm's length, unawares that by doing so, I most likely did you, my dear students, a disservice. But aren't we always wiser with hindsight?

"I now understand that in shielding myself from the pain of my past, I have missed opportunities to connect with each of you on a deeper level, to share in your joys and sorrows, and to truly understand the remarkable individuals you were becoming.

"The turning point in my perception happened during the war

years, and in the aftermath, when I received word of the incredible courage displayed by six of my former students, all of them here tonight. Esther, Anna, Sable, Edda, Océane, and Lili—each of you joined the resistance movements of World War II in different corners of Europe, risking your lives to fight against tyranny and oppression.

"Your bravery and selflessness have left an inextinguishable mark on my heart, and tonight, I feel so very honored to be able to celebrate your extraordinary accomplishments in my school and show the very last cohort of students that a Le Manoir diploma can lead to so much more than the smooth running of a great household.

"But before celebrating my star pupils, I feel compelled to share with you the story of my own life, and the mistakes I made along the way. For it is in facing our past, in acknowledging our shortcomings and failings, that we find the courage to forge a new path forward.

"My life's journey began in 1896, in Vienna. I was born into a Jewish family whose world was steeped in tradition and culture, where the scent of fresh challah wafted through our home on Shabbat evenings, and the sound of my father's voice reciting ancient prayers filled the air."

She paused again, searching out Esther's eyes in the front row. Esther leaned forward, so as not to miss one word. The hand that held Tore's was trembling. Elsie seemed to be trembling as well but soon collected herself again, after a reverent glance at Anna.

"My father was a prominent businessman and philanthropist, so I was raised amidst the splendor of a city teeming with intellect and

creativity. Both my parents, Nathaniel and Leah Goldschmidt, were
pillars of our community, known for their generosity and kindness.
Our home was a haven of warmth and love, where the laughter of
children and the aroma of home-cooked meals filled every corner."

A SMILE PLAYED around the corners of Elsie's mouth at the sweet
memories of her youth. Esther perched even further on the edge of
her chair. Of course, the Weiss's knew the Goldschmidts! They had
frequented the same circles.

Elsie continued her monologue, seeming more withdrawn now,
the smile evaporated. Her audience sat breathless, wondering what
she would share next. Madame Paul, a Jewess? Nothing had ever
pointed in that direction. On the contrary, she had isolated the
Jewish students before the war, denigrated them.

"As the shadows of World War I loomed over Europe, our once
vibrant Viennese society began to crumble. In the chaos of the war
in 1915, I found myself thrust into an arranged marriage with Paul
Vierret, a Swiss businessman based in Lausanne. It was a union
born of necessity, a means of securing my family's safety and
protecting our assets in turbulent times.

"For two years, I played the role of the dutiful wife, outwardly
supporting my husband's business endeavors while harboring
doubts and fears about the morality of his actions. Our union
remained childless, though my husband's various mistresses
apparently produced enough illegitimate offspring.

"Then, a sudden welcome opportunity came on my path at the end
of 1917. My predecessor here at Le Manoir, a lady from Bern called
Madame Veronica Brisancourt, suddenly passed away in November
1917 and as it was at the height of the war, the board searched for a

suitable candidate to keep the school going. My husband bought the position for me for a sum of Swiss francs he didn't want to disclose to me. It was the only kind gesture he ever did for me, though it was not without scruples, of course."

Elsie laughed but there was little joy in her tone.

"From the very first day, I absolutely adored this job, as if it was made for me. And it was a welcome escape from a loveless marriage. I threw my heart and soul into it and when the war ended in 1918, Le Manoir was on the rise to becoming the top-grade finishing school in all of Switzerland."

She paused again, peered into the audience as if asking for help. There was some shuffling and soft coughing, but then she continued.

"Through it all, I mostly feel a profound sense of remorse for the role I have played in shaping the lives of my students here at Le Manoir. For too long, I believed the only way to maintain order and discipline was to enforce rules and regulations, to put students in their place, in what may have been an unfriendly manner. I have favored some over others, turned a blind eye to injustices, and allowed my own biases and fears to cloud my judgment.

"I must also acknowledge that I have been complicit in perpetuating a system of privilege and inequality. For years, I accepted large sums of money as tuition fees from well-to-do families, turning a blind eye to the indiscretions of their daughters in exchange for financial gain. In doing so, I betrayed the trust placed in me as the headmistress of this esteemed institution. And for that I am truly sorry and will fully accept my punishment when I meet my Maker.

"Outside the school, in the background, was always my unhappy marriage which deteriorated at the same rate as Europe descended into darkness once again, with the rise of Nazi Germany and the spread of anti-Semitic sentiments. In the 1930s, I found myself torn between loyalty to my family and the growing realization I could no longer turn a blind eye to the injustices around me.

"And yet, I did. I was so afraid the Board would expose my Jewish background, that I did everything to hide it. Out of cowardice, I put a dagger in my own heart as I started spreading those heinous anti-Semitic sentiments myself. I broke with my own family back in Austria..."

Now it was Edda who sat straight and pale as a statue. How she remembered the collaboration of her parents with the Nazis and what it had led to. She stared at her former schoolmistress with disbelief but not without a degree of compassion. If there was one person in the room who understood the horns of the collaboration dilemma, it was a descendent of the Van der Valk Barony.

"I learned in June 1945 that both my parents and my two brothers, Aaron and Levi, with at least twenty other family members were all killed in Nazi concentration camps."

A wave of horror and dismay went through the crowd. Elsie sat still, her head bowed, staring down at her white ringless fingers intertwined in her lap.

"I know. Some of you here in the audience have suffered the same losses. We cannot come to terms with it and yet we go on. We live on. God knows why. But my fate didn't end there.

"It was in the same month I finally got word about my family that my husband was arrested. Little did I know, or perhaps little did I *want* to know, about his involvement in the illicit trade of stolen Jewish art and jewelry, which he started even before the Second World War.

"He apparently acquired these treasures through clandestine channels, exploiting the chaos of war to line his own pockets. The origins of these stolen artifacts are shrouded in secrecy, but I suspect they were pilfered from the homes and possessions of innocent victims of the Nazi regime.

"In his greed, my husband sold these precious heirlooms to wealthy buyers, both within and beyond Europe's borders. I was blinded by my own desire to be blind, but also in all honesty didn't know the full extent of his crimes until his arrest. The Swiss police informed me of what had taken place in our house. Until my dying day, I will seek redemption for the role I unwittingly played in his misdeeds by not looking more closely."

She took another sip of water and as she placed the glass back on the table let out a deep sigh. Then smiled again as if the sun broke free from the clouds that had obscured her view.

"Fear not, esteemed guests, I will not take up your whole evening with the litany of my sins. We're coming to the end of it and then the true celebration can begin. In recent years, I found the courage to confront my past and reclaim my identity. I divorced Paul Vierret, but until this anniversary, continued to use his name because that is how everyone knew me at Le Manoir.

"But as of today, I reclaim my maiden name and wear it with pride. I am Elsie Goldschmidt. No more, no less.

"I've made the decision to close Le Manoir as a finishing school this summer and transform it into a sanctuary for Holocaust survivors and refugees, a place where they can find solace and healing in the aftermath of tragedy.

"With this new direction in my life, I'm honored to step in my late father's footsteps as a modest philanthropist. The house will be renamed *Manoir de L'Espoir*. Manor of Hope.

"I will take up residence at Manoir de L'Espoir permanently. The quarters where I now have my office and the two adjacent rooms, will be turned into a studio for me to live in. I so love the view from my office over the lake with the Savoy Alps in the distance. That view never fails to fill my heart with joy and tranquillity.

"I sincerely hope that instead of being a school mistress, I will be able to serve my new guests in humility and gratitude for the remaining years of my life."

Elsie rose, still smiling but with tears glistening in her eyes. Her audience also rose, already starting to applaud, but she silenced them with a gesture that was still very much Madame Paul. Listen and obey. The fortitude of that gesture made the Resistance Girls grin in recognition.

"Can I have your attention for just one more minute, please? As I stand here before you tonight, I want you to understand that it is partly through the challenges and struggles of my own life that I have come to understand the true meaning of courage and resilience.

"The other part comes from the stories of the eight Resistance Girls here in our midst. Two from the first war and six from the second. "

"The latter part of this evening will be in their honor, but as we are about to rearrange the stage for a surprise I have for them, we'll take a thirty-minute break. There are refreshments and music by the Alpine Harmony Quartet. All four members of this sublime quartet are Holocaust survivors and dear, dear friends. Can I have a round of applause for Eva Bernstein on the violin, Isaac Cohen on Cello, Rachel Stein on Viola, and David Klein on Violin?"

The entire audience burst into applause. The musicians, dressed in professional black with accents of white, rose and bowed to them before returning to strumming their instruments.

Despite the school mistress's request to applaud the Resistance Girls, the entire crowd cheered as much for Elsie Goldschmidt, who'd finally become an ordinary mortal, a warm and caring person, a headmistress they'd judged so wrongly themselves. But how could they have known what was behind that austere façade? They couldn't.

AND THROUGH EIGHT heads went the thought, *What on earth could be a surprise after that reveal?*

18

THE REFRESHMENT BREAK

In the intermission, tall glasses of lemonade and delicate apricot pastries were passed around, filling the air with a sweet aroma that mingled with the strains of the Alpine Harmony Quartet's music.

As the melodies of Beethoven, Mozart, and Brahms drifted through the room, interwoven with haunting pieces by Shostakovich and Weinberg, the atmosphere was infused with a sense of reverence and reflection.

The Resistance Girls, gathered in small clusters together with their husbands, shared in soft-spoken conversations. As the quartet's music continued to weave its spell, they reflected on Elsie's revelations with expressions of wonder and curiosity.

"I would never have guessed," Madeleine professed to daughter Lili, her voice tinged with a hint of shame. "All those years, and we had no idea what she was going through. You and I were quite little horrors, weren't we?"

"Maman, as you just said, we didn't know! But do you think we would have behaved better if we had?"

"Not ye, *mo leannan,* ye'd created a racket anywhere if ye could," Iain commented in his Scottish brogue, his arm lovingly around his wife's waist." Lili looked up at him, her red hair gleaming in the light of the chandeliers.

"Oh you," she giggled, "you've quite type casted me, haven't you? I suppose I must be glad you just called me your darling instead of Scottish Gaelic for 'wild woman'."

Agnès, who stood nearby with Alan at her side, mainly listened in to the conversation around her, as she had no recollections about Le Manoir to share herself, but her friend Madeleine wanted to know her opinion anyway.

"It's incredible," the kind-hearted Agnès agreed. "To think a woman of her stature and so prominently in the public eye hid so much from the world, all to protect herself and her family. She must feel so deeply that she failed them."

"She seems to be making the necessary amends," Gerry, Madeleine's husband, who always longed for people to do the right thing, chimed in. "Everyone deserves a second chance, don't you agree, Maddy?"

"You gave me one, so yes!" Madeleine winked. "What about you Alan? What do you make of this quizzical finishing school and its mistress?"

Alan laughed heartily. "I'm not sure I'm entitled to any opinion on the matter as I'm clearly an outsider. In the States, we call these places 'charm schools,' which sounds perhaps even odder than a finishing school. Océane had an alright time here, I suppose. I do love the surroundings."

"Don't be so darn correct, beating around the bush, Doctor Bell," Madeleine teased him. "Tell us what you think of the former Madame Paul."

"Ah, I see. Now that is an interesting phenomenon. She definitely went through a paradigm change. It's food for psychiatrists.

Of which the Swiss have plenty of excellent practitioners. In laymen terms I'd say, she'll get there. She is on the right path."

Nearby, Edda and Anna exchanged knowing glances, their expressions a mixture of sadness and understanding. "She must have been under such tremendous pressure," Edda remarked, her voice filled with empathy. "To keep such a heavy burden hidden for so long."

Anna nodded, her eyes misting over with emotion. "It makes you wonder how little we really know about people. Their motives, their inner drive, their past."

Ash seemed rather agitated by his wife's former school mistress's words.

"The Swiss have been so good at helping us, survivors of the Holocaust, immediately after the war, but I wonder how many of them gave their support because they knew what had happened in their so-called neutral country. The Nazis made good use of that neutrality and the Swiss and their banks weren't averse to making serious money. They were notorious for fencing stolen art and jewellery that passed through their country. Not just goods, money-laundering happened on a large scale as well. Millions of Jewish money."

"Very true," Henryk spoke up, "so many Jewish prisoners in Sachsenhausen told me their houses were pilfered even before they were sent to the ghettos and then the last of their things were ripped off them when they arrived in the camps."

Anna sighed. It always hurt when Henryk talked of his time in the concentration camps, and now she was face to face with another survivor, Edda's Asher. Such a proud and beautiful man, but with a hard scorn on his face right now. Of all the people in the room he seemed to have most difficulty forgiving Elsie and who could blame him?

Across the room, Esther and Sable were deep in conversation

with their husbands, their voices low and earnest as they discussed the implications of Elsie's revelations.

"If I'd ever have guessed what she was involved in while she was just like me, a well-to-do Jewish Viennese, I'd have stood up more for myself." Esther's green eyes flickered intensely, her brow furrowed in anger. "Of course, I know the Goldschmidts and so would Asher. But then again, who am I to judge? I'm just glad I never had to walk one mile in her shoes. I think I would have killed myself."

"No, *Jeger*, you wouldn't have," Tore corrected his wife while looking at her with ardent admiration. "A girl like you would've never made the choices she made. You'd have killed the husband with your own hands."

"Hush, Tore, don't say these things. I'm not proud of what I had to do during the war." She knew he was referring to how she'd shot Harald Rinnan after the Quisling supporter had deported her family.

Sable came between them, her expression somber. "You are right though, Es. Let's be glad *we did what we did* during the war and ended up on the right side of history."

Bill, who'd kept silent so far, made a gesture showing he wanted to say something. Not a man of many words, they all waited to hear what he had to say.

The two former SOE agents, Bill and Tore, liked and respected each other to the core and shared a temperament that knew how to cut the frills and get to the point.

"Not many people would've had the guts to do what Elsie Gold-schmidt just did. She needn't have. Yet, she invited us to witness her transformation. I will not forget this evenin' as long as I live. I'd say three hurrahs for Elsie Goldsmidth and her Manor de L'Espoir, or whatever she calls it."

Esther, her eyes suddenly alight with enthusiasm, turned to

Tore, her voice barely audible over the music. "I'm just thinking aloud. Could we perhaps create some sort of collaboration between Elsie's house for refugees and our recuperation center? We could offer therapy and skiing lessons to Holocaust survivors, provide them with a sense of healing and hope."

Tore nodded thoughtfully, his gaze lingering on the quartet as they played. "It's an interesting idea," he replied, "but what about the distance? It's not like we are next-door to each other."

"But darling," Esther would not be stopped now, "in our center we've already seen the healing power of recreation and therapy first-hand. We have so much expertise we could offer her. If we can extend our knowledge to those who have suffered so greatly, it would be a profound service."

MEANWHILE, the current and former students of Le Manoir sauntered back to their seats as the music had stopped and a bell rang, like in the old school days. They suddenly remembered Elsie had said she had a surprise for them...

19

MADAME DOCTEUR

A hush fell over the theatre as the audience settled back into their seats, the soft murmur of conversation and the rustle of clothes ebbing away. Anticipation hummed through the air like an electric current.

All eyes were on the quartet with their instruments poised and their bows ready to strike the first note of the next portion of the evening.

The moment of silence stretched, a pregnant vacuum in between two worlds, yet filled with the echo of expectation, until the first notes of Beethoven's 5th Symphony crashed through the air.

The familiar da-da-da-dum motif rang out, bold and resolute, occupying the entire hall with a sense of urgency and purpose.

The melody unfolded, weaving its way into their ears like a thread of premonition, each note building upon the last with mounting intensity.

As the quartet played on and the music swelled, the Resistance Girls exchanged puzzled glances, their hearts beating hard, in time with the rhythm of the music. Beside them, their husbands leaned forward in their seats, caught up in the energy of the moment as the music drove toward a climactic crescendo.

And then, just as the tension reached its peak, the curtains parted, revealing eight figures seated on stage alongside Elsie. Next to each person stood an empty chair.

The final notes of the movement rang out, lingering in the air like a benediction, as the audience erupted into applause, their spirits lifted by the stirring melody and the promise of what was to come.

Each of the eight individuals, unknown to most but intimately connected to one woman in the audience, represented the courage and selflessness of the Resistance Girls.

Elsie stood up and grasped the microphone, her voice ringing out clear and steady in the silence that followed.

"Mesdames et Messieurs, it is my honor and privilege to introduce to you eight war survivors," she began, her words carrying the weight of emotion. "Each of these mystery guests represents countless lives saved by the extraordinary Resistance women seated in your midst today."

The atmosphere in the audience crackled with astonishment and joy as the reality of the scene in front of them sunk in. Faces lit up with smiles, tears glistened in eyes, and hearts swelled with pride as the magnitude of Elsie's surprise became clear.

Husbands put arms around wives, who were overwhelmed with emotion.

But for the eight Resistance women, everyone, including the nine people on stage, stood up and began a standing ovation that lasted minutes.

It was almost too much to bear, as the tribute was also larded with tears for those the women hadn't been able to save.

The sight of these beloved individuals, whose lives they had touched and who had touched theirs in ways so profound and life-saving, was almost too much to handle.

They exchanged incredulous glances, their hands reaching out to grasp one another's in a silent gesture of solidarity and shared astonishment.

They sat like that as Elsie continued,

"I would like to invite the Resistance Girls on stage. Please take your seats next to the person you saved. We will then hear their stories from the mouths of the survivors."

Kisses and hugs were exchanged between husbands and wives before Agnès, Madeleine, Lili, Océane, Esther, Sable, Edda, and Anna walked up the steps to the stage.

The quartet accompanied their final victory march by playing Bach's "Jesu, Joy of Man's Desiring.". The iconic piece had a gentle, uplifting melody that complemented the moment, conveying a sense of reverence and celebration as the girls progressed towards their special person on stage.

The serene music created a meaningful, emotional moment.

Embracing their special person, tears flooded freely, followed by cries of incredulity, *Is it really **you**? What are **you** doing here? How did **you** come here?*

"Please sit down, everyone, and let me explain the background to this surprise, which is really my present to you." Elsie spoke, her own voice thick with emotion for what she saw happening before her. All eyes turned to the schoolmistress, moist and elated eyes, while a deep thank-you rose from their throats as one.

"This is what is about to happen. I will hand the microphone to the first person and he will explain who he is and how Doctor Agnès de Dragoncourt-Bell saved his life. When he has shared his story, he will hand the microphone to the next survivor and so on."

Elsie handed the microphone to a man in a faded, old-fashioned, blue aviation uniform that practically burst at the seams but was richly hung with a plethora of medals and ribbons.

The audience was still as if spellbound. The middle-aged man hesitated a moment, clearly not accustomed to being in the limelight at a finishing school in Switzerland.

His brown eyes, under a graying mop of thick hair, sought those of Agnès and as soon as he focused on her, his reservation melted away and a big smile lit up his face from under an impressive moustache.

Taking off his cap, he placed it on his knee and his big hands grabbed the microphone with force.

"*Messieurs et Mesdames*," he began, first hesitantly but then gaining confidence, bowing his head reverently for Agnès, "but in particular *Madame Docteur*. It is an honor to be invited here today to celebrate the incredible courage of these women before you.

"I was kindly invited by Madame Elsie Goldschmidt to share a small but significant part of my life's story with you. A story that would have ended in an early grave, like the millions of my contemporaries, had it not been for the remarkable interception by *Madame Docteur*.

"My name is *Capitaine Jerôme Heurtier*, and though I now sit before you as a man nearing fifty, there was a time when I was but a young pilot, full of dreams and aspirations. I'm talking about the period before the Great War, when aviation was still in its infancy.

"I hail from Marseilles, where my father owned a modest grocery store on the *Rue Pardis*. From a young age, I helped in the shop and to this day I run "*Épicerie Paradis*" with my wife Eugenie.

"But as a young lad, my heart didn't yearn for cabbages and bottles of milk. This heart…," he bumped a forceful fist on his chest that made the medals dance and chink, "… this heart yearned for adventure. When war came to France in 1914, I wanted nothing but serve my country, and I enlisted with the 2nd Infantry Division. Little did I know then that my path would lead me to the skies, to the world of aviation.

"After training at *Issoudun Aerodrome*, I was assigned to MS38, a Morane-Saulnier squadron, as an observer," he chuckled at the memory, looked straight at the audience.

"I must be boring you. These days nobody flies Morane-Saulniers anymore, but in my day and age they were the height of technology. Anyway, I promise this won't take long and I'll get to *Madame Docteur's* healing hands soon enough.

"All this is but a roundabout way to say I wasn't just an amateur who fell from the sky during my first flight. You see, I was a bit of a showman at the time. Germany had the Red Baron and France had me, *Le Marchand Volant*, the Flying Merchant."

His grin was infectious, and the audience had no problem picturing the now-portly, but very lively, pilot to have been a daredevil of the skies in his early years.

"In 1916, I finally became a fighter pilot, flying Nieuports. Ha, I engaged in many an aerial combat with the enemy, among them the

Red Baron! I earned fifteen victories before luck turned against me during the Spring Offensive over the Somme region. Shot down by a German bomber, my left leg splintered, I was heavily wounded and given up for dead by my squadron." The brown eyes turned almost black but sought the blue gaze of his rescuer. "It was then, in the midst of my darkest hour, that *Madame Docteur* didn't give up on me.

"Her skilful hands saved my leg and my gut, though she later explained to me she had to do something she'd never done before and that the operation often failed to do the trick. But she did it. And I can walk and waltz with my wife. I can even fly a plane if you let me. So, I tell you folks, this slender lady, she was just in her early twenties, but had a willpower to save lives I've never again encountered in my life. Or it must have been that co-surgeon of hers, who wasn't her husband at the time. *Docteur Bell*, also present here. Man, if you thought us soldiers and flyers had it tough. I've seen them go into the makeshift operation room at six in the morning and still be at work after midnight. Those two saved lives. Not one, not ten, not a hundred, but thousands.

"And let me tell you one more thing about this dear lady, who apparently is also a Baroness. She was not just a surgeon, but a guardian angel, guiding me and all these other sorry sights of men back from the brink of despair."

People rose to clap, but Capitaine Heurtier shouted "Wait!" in the microphone with such loudness the room instantly fell still again.

"After that war, our paths crossed twice, but haven't again in many years. I was graciously invited by General Ferdinand Foch to pin her Médaille Commémorative de la Guerre 1914–1918 on her chest. It was a moment of profound gratitude and remembrance. I'll never forget. You may think me showing off with my brass," he pointed to his own chest. "But *Madame Docteur* has certainly as many in her drawer. French, British, and American medals, you name it. And so very deserved!

"The last time we met I took her for a spin through the air in my Nieuport. I think she enjoyed it and I promise I flew as if I was transporting a crate of precious crystal glasses. No loops, no spins. And I put her back on solid ground with the softest landing I ever made. True?"

Agnès smiled and said in the microphone he held to her mouth, "very true! It was fantastic. My very first flight. I'll never forget it." Heurtier continued, his voice a bit shaky now.

"I can sound a bit rough around the edges but this invitation, this moment moves me perhaps more than anything else in my life. Time has passed, we've had another war, in which I was grateful to be an instructor to the young flying aces. But today, on this special night, I am here for all the hundreds of wounded soldiers whose lives *Madame Docteur* saved. Her compassion, her skill, and her unwavering dedication to duty are a testament to the goodness of the human spirit in the face of adversity.

"I am forever grateful for her bravery, her kindness, and her tireless efforts to heal the wounds of war. *Madame Docteur*, you are a true hero, and I am honored to have crossed paths with you in this life. Thank you."

Agnès felt a lump form in her throat as she returned his salute, her eyes brimming with tears of recognition and remembrance.

In that moment, surrounded by the echoes of their shared past, she felt a deep sense of gratitude for the man whose life she had saved, preserving his legs and his future.

As the audience looked on, the power of the moment was palpable in the air. For Agnès and Capitaine Heurtier, reunited after so many years, it was a moment of closure and catharsis, a chance to honor the bonds forged in the crucible of war and the spirit of resilience and hope that had carried them through.

The audience was allowed to clap until Capitaine Heurtier handed the microphone to the next mystery guest, who was at least known to some people in the audience and who came for Madeleine.

Countess Elle de Dragoncourt, Madeleine's eldest sister.

20

ERNST HÖBEL STRIKES BACK

Countess Elle de Dragoncourt had aged gracefully. She still wore her hair in a thick brown braid down her back, as she had done for decades.

She still had a tomboyish, lean figure, tall and strong, with her tough-girl exterior, piercing topaz eyes, red nails and a pointed chin that was always slightly tilted, as if saying, "show me what you got."

A revered female racecar driver with many Grand Prix records to her name, among them 24 Heurs du Mans and the South African Grand Prix in her loyal speed monster, a 2 liter-supercharged Bugatti.

A resident of New York for many years with her friend and partner, Abigail McAllister, she'd flown back to Europe on the request of the headmistress of Le Manoir.

"Ladies and gentlemen, as some of you know I am no stranger to this hall, nor to my family in the audience. At least, I hope not!

"I was a student here at Le Manoir when the former headmistress,

Madame Brisancourt, still held sway. A quick calculation will tell you how old that makes me! But for those who don't know me, I'm Elle de Dragoncourt, Madeleine's eldest sister."

The audience laughed, some with recognition, others in astonishment, that these two tall, poplar-like women were indeed sisters.

"I come before you here not technically as having been saved by my sister, as she didn't pull me out of the wreckage of our Château with her bare hands, but to tell you that if it hadn't been for my reckless baby sister, the people who were trapped inside our summer residence near the Somme River would probably all have died. Let me explain." She grabbed her sister's hand and squeezed it affectionately.

"This tale goes back a long way, to the waning months of the First World War, the summer of 1918. A summer so hot and so sultry that it should have been heaven on earth. But it was hell, absolute hell. The Entente Powers, as we called the Allied forces then, had lost almost 6 million soldiers in a trench war against Imperial Germany. A front in Belgium and France that shifted a few kilometers back and forth, was right on the doorstep of my family's summer residence, Châtau de Dragoncourt.

"As a whole generation of French and Commonwealth young men were mowed down by machine guns and mustard gas, Agnès and Alan and their team fought around the clock to save as many of them as they could.

"I was an ambulance driver during the entire time we lived near the front. I like driving like nothing else, as some of you here might know," Elle grinned and holding her hands before her as if gripping a steering wheel. "But I can tell you those hundreds of bumpy rides from the trenches, transporting maimed and howling soldiers in the back, was the hardest thing I've done in my entire life.

"But wait, I didn't come here to tell you about *my* challenges, but how I became a witness to the pluck of my remarkable sis, whom we used to call Mad-Maddy. And everywhere Mad-Maddy went, her pet monkey LouLou went with her. Only, not on this one trip that I'm going to tell you about.

"So, you get the picture, our ancestral home, Château de Dragoncourt, stood as a bastion of hope in the middle of the chaos of battle. We were on French soil still, at least until 1918, and we ran a makeshift operating room in our former dining room and one of the wings had been turned into a ward.

"The floor of the great entrance hall was filled with stretchers and our Versailles-style gardens dotted with recuperating soldiers in wheelchairs and nurses in white aprons." Elle paused a moment, her topaz gaze fixing the audience as if wanting to make sure they got the picture etched in their mind's eye.

"Oh, I forgot to mention we also had a batch of very attractive and fierce looking Brits under the command of Major Gerald Hamilton, staying under our roof. His troops were very poshly called the Royal West Kent Regiment and they donned stunning uniforms and sensational mustaches.

"The commander in question is now Maddy's husband. Let me ask my sister this out straight now, as I've never asked her before. Did you or did you not pull your prank to win Gerry's heart?" Elle looked straight at her sister.

Madeleine laughed out loud, "I did not. Well, maybe a tiny bit."

"Alright that sets the record straight. I'm digressing too much, but I'm getting there. The Germans were approaching. We were losing terrain. And then my twin brother Jacques, who's here somewhere in the audience..."

Elle waved a long arm and Jacques called back, "I'll catch you both later!"

"Anyway, I think it was Jacques who said there was a secret tunnel underneath our Château that ran halfway underground to Amines. It dated from the time when our forefathers were Huguenots and needed to protect themselves from Catholics with pitchforks. We showed that tunnel to Major Gerald, and Madeleine was there as well. Only the medical staff stayed back at the hospital while we explored.

"And then – lo and behold – as we were exploring the tunnel, we got word Dragoncourt had been attacked by the Germans and there was no way we could go back without being taken prisoner. We tried to backtrack, but they had locked the tunnel door from the inside, which we had deliberately left open to be able to return. We were forced to flee and stay at a hotel in Amiens that was run by friends of our parents. All we could do was wait and see what would happen. Well, of course the worst happened. The Germans took control of Dragoncourt and the medics were their prisoners of war.

"But never underestimate Mad-Maddy. Armed with an iron will to get back into the Château to retrieve the spare key, she put on the uniform of a deceased Prussian soldier and called herself Corporal Ernst Höbel, who had a message from General Von Spitzenburg stationed in Roye for Major-General Eberhard Graf von Spiegler, who was in command of Dragoncourt now.

"Madeleine ventured into the heart of the enemy's stronghold, which was our rightful home, her red locks cut very short, and a crude moustache drawn upon her face with coal. Speaking in gruff German, she bluffed her way past the suspicions of Von Spiegler, seizing the key to our salvation and unlocking the path to freedom, returning through the tunnel to us in Amiens. You should have seen that grinning face of hers. We were shocked, not only by her changed exterior but by the sheer audacity of her actions."

Elle paused for a moment, again squeezing Madeleine's hand, who was grinning the way she had done on that August morning in 1918. She finished her story quickly.

"There is an anecdote related to this, which Madeleine didn't know at the time. Through a twist of fate that binds our destinies in ways we sometimes cannot fathom, Major-General Von Spiegler bore a connection to our dear Agnès, a connection that only deepened the significance of Madeleine's actions.

"With unyielding determination, she not only seized the key to our group's personal salvation, but also paved the way for the Allies to liberate the area through that same tunnel and take the Germans by surprise. Maddy also made sure she brought about the downfall of that horrid man, Von Spiegler, and the end of his hideous reign."

The audience was very silent. Clearly deeply impressed by Madeleine's audacious actions.

She seemed such a lady, she *was* a lady, and yet that mischievous glint in her eye betrayed a fearless soul and a limitless love for home and family.

Elle stood up and addressed her family in the audience,

"please Jacques, Marielle, Daphne, and Paul, will you come on stage to celebrate with us the freedom Maddy battled for in her own unique way?"

They all saw a tall, distinguished, gray-haired man, a beautiful Italian Contessa, dark-haired Daphne with her Congolese husband step onto the stage.

Daphne, in particular, in a sunflower dress with wide skirt, and her husband wearing a tie of the same pattern, drew all eyes towards them.

They were famous heroes of World War 2 and now the couture team at DragonBâh Chic. Everyone gasped at seeing them.

But they came for Tante Madeleine, and they all went to stand around her. She rose, a bit shaky with emotion, and received their embrace with tears in her eyes.

"*Merci beaucoup!* Thank you, darlings. I'd do it again if I had to. You know I can't stay out of mischief no matter how I try." And then she said in the microphone, "and thank you, Gerry, for always believing in me, and for my children."

And her eyes went to the young girl who'd sat next to her during Elle's tribute.

"That's right," Elle took the microphone back from Madeleine. "It's now my job to introduce the next mystery guest. Please welcome Sarah Goldmunz-Hamilton."

21

CHOPIN'S PRELUDE IN C MINOR

W hen the microphone was handed to Sarah Goldmunz-Hamilton, silence fell over the hall. All eyes were drawn to the beautiful young woman, who sat there with such grace and poise.

Who was she? Clearly part of Madeleine and Lili's family, but how and why?

Sarah had dark wavy hair, so unlike the ginger in her mother's and sister's hair. Her long ponytail was held together with a simple pink ribbon, the same color as her dress.

But it was her face that captivated all attention, a face so finely featured she resembled an Italian Renaissance painting.

And yet the graveness of that face with the luminous brown eyes and set mouth lacked any of the humor the earlier two speakers had possessed.

Her expression was almost mask-like, but everyone could see she could barely control the emotions raging beneath that smooth surface.

With a gentle grace beyond her eighteen years, Sarah addressed the gathered crowd, her voice soft and trembling.

"Good evening, everyone," she began, the dark eyes scanning the faces before her until they settled on Lili at her side. Her savior, her sister, her guardian angel. Sarah's pale skin glowed in the stage lights as she struggled for words.

"My name is Sarah Goldmunz-Hamilton." She looked to Lili for help, who encouraged her with a firm nod.
"Please forgive me if my stumbling over words doesn't express what I want to say. It is hard for me to talk about the past."

She paused again, looking like a lost little girl. The little girl she'd been during the war. Lili grabbed her hand and held it firmly.
"I'm here, darling," she whispered in the distraught girl's ear. Sarah took heart from Lili's encouragement and though her hand holding the microphone still trembled, she spoke up a little louder.

"I was ten years old when Belgium surrendered to Nazi Germany in the spring of 1940. I was living with my grandparents Isaac and Elizabeth Goldmunz on the Rubenslei in Antwerp because my parents had gone to Paris on what they said was 'business'. You see, my family has been in the diamond industry for generations. I think it was my great-grandfather who settled in Antwerp before the First World War, but... but I'm not sure anymore... I know my family was in England in the Interbellum, but I don't know the details, only that my father was born there..." The big eyes went in search of Lili again, who gave her another encouraging nod.

"Anyway, of course we knew Hitler hated Jews, so we were far from happy when the Nazis came to Antwerp, and I think my parents being in Paris for an extended time had something to do with that as well. But I'm not sure.

"My grandfather was a very wise and very brave man, and he said that I shouldn't be afraid and hold my head high and be a true Goldmunz. I tried but I was afraid most days, as the German soldiers who now marched through our city were far from friendly. They harassed Jews... uh... I saw that often. And school wasn't much fun anymore. Many friends had left the country. They went to France, or even to America, and I hoped we would go too. Or at least that we would go to Paris to Mama and Papa. But then Paris also fell to Hitler, and Grandpapa said my parents had gone to Bordeaux in the south of France."

Sarah swallowed, biting back her tears. She didn't need to add she hadn't understood the family dynamics at the time.

The questions on her mind were palpable to all who listened to her story. The questions a ten-year-old hadn't dared to ask and now never would have the answers to. But Sarah continued her sad tale.

"Then something very nice happened in my life. Lili came to our house one night. I didn't know who she was, but she was very pretty and very British. When she told me she'd come on the Golden Arrow, I was so excited. We had taken the same train ferry between Calais and Dover before the war. You know, as a family. It was so wonderful to talk with Lili. To talk about England. I often dreamed of living in England, far away from Hitler..."

Sarah's words trailed off, and for a moment her face took on a dreamy expression.

"In the first years of my life I enjoyed a happy and stable childhood, living in a nice neighborhood in Antwerp surrounded by my family. Though I was an only child, we always had children in the house and there was always food and laughter and lots of love. My Great Aunt Agatha also lived with us after her husband died. But there was plenty of space in our house. It was really big with at least ten bedrooms and three bathrooms.

"We also traveled a lot because of the family business, and I was taken along since I was a little girl. I remember going to Paris to the Jardin de Tuileries often, and the merry-go-round on the Brighton Palace Pier. Grandpapa and Grandmama had lived in Brighton when my father, Jacob, was born. We even once sailed for ten days from Hamburg to New York on the SS Manhattan and stayed in New York in an apartment looking out over Central Park." Soon her voice trembled again with the weight of memories too heavy to bear.

"I recently heard that the same SS Manhattan was used for the "Kindertransport" in 1939, to bring German Jewish children without their parents from Hamburg to safety in England. But of course, in those happy days in the 1930s, I had no idea I, too, would become an orphan.

"Life was already completely changing when Lili came, but we still had food and Grandpapa was consulted by the Germans about the diamond industry. I guess because he was the President of the *Bourse Diamantaire Anversoise*, you know, someone important in the diamond business. Grandmama assured me we would be alright, and the Germans wouldn't dare to do anything to us."

Sarah's voice faltered and she looked apologetically at Lili.

"Am I rambling, Lili? Please do tell me. I'm so lost in my story of what to tell everyone?"

"You're doing fine, darling. Everyone is listening. They want to hear it all," Lili assured her sister.

"Grandmama told me I could show my room to Lili. I remember being very shy, but glad to leave the dining room and go upstairs. As every night, there were also Germans coming to dinner at our house and they made me feel so uncomfortable."

Sarah's eyes darkened.

"Much later I learned they actually came to check on my grandfather's every move. He was technically their prisoner already and they just used him because of his expertise. They all acted very jolly and friendly, but I felt the tension. I felt something was very wrong already then, so I was glad when Lili took my hand and we escaped to my room. Lili was so nice. I truly thought her a princess, or something. She had such nice clothes and perfect manners. Nothing like my clumsiness or timidness."

Sarah took the audience on a journey back in time, to the moment when she and Lili retreated to the sanctuary of her room, seeking solace from the chaos in her head and heart.

"I think Lili liked my room. I liked it tremendously myself, especially in those days when I felt so unsafe. It was a room filled with dolls, picture books, and of course my piano." She smiled at the memory. "My room had a cream carpet that covered the wooden floor, a beautiful white bedspread draped over a golden bedframe, and the white piano standing proudly against one wall. I think I liked white a lot those days. Though I loved pink too. I remember wearing a pink dress that day, so I thought I'd put on one today as well."

Sarah's voice was now filled with warmth and nostalgia.

"I think we were friends then already though there was eleven years
between us. I called her Miss Lili, just to be sure, but it felt like
having a big sister. I felt so proud and so grown-up in her presence.
Then we read together and lost ourselves in the world of Mary
Poppins and her whimsical adventures."

As she spoke, Sarah's dark eyes sparkled with fond memories,
her heart so clearly full of gratitude for the kindness and love she'd
found in Lili's presence.

"All I really wanted was to play the piano for her, but I didn't feel I
was good enough yet. I had been practicing Chopin's Prelude in C
Minor and my piano teacher Mademoiselle Cohen had said I had
almost grasped it. But I had no lessons anymore as Mademoiselle
Cohen was no longer in Antwerp. I don't know where she was. One
day when I went to the "Muziekschool" with my music books, two
Germans stood in front of the door and told me to go home. I was
almost sick with worry and missing Mademoiselle Cohen, who had
been my piano teacher for four years. And I missed the lessons."

Sarah looked around her with an uncertain look on her solemn
young face.

"I feel I'm rambling all the time. Let me try to go faster. Lili left again
and then I missed her too. I missed my parents. I missed
Mademoiselle Cohen, and I missed my friends from school, and
now I also missed Lili. But Lili came back. Several times. At the time
I didn't know what her role was, but I understood she was doing
business for my grandfather."

Sarah stopped and the gaze she gave Lili held all the admiration in the world.

"Lili did extremely dangerous work. As the war lasted longer and grew grimmer, my grandfather understood it was a matter of time before the Germans would take complete control of the Antwerp diamond industry and his position would no longer be needed by them. So, Lili was our diamond courier.
She smuggled precious diamonds out of Belgium and brought them to safety at the London Syndicate, until..."

Sarah took a deep breath,

"... until ...it was three years later and there was a lot of commotion in the house. Grandmama helped me pack a bag and just said it was better if I went to England with Lili. But she was so rushed and unlike her normal joyful self that I didn't want to leave. I begged my family to come with me and they promised they would come with Lili the next time. All of them, also Mama and Papa, about whom we hadn't heard anything for over a year. Maybe that was really the plan. I think it must have been. But everything went wrong."

Sarah could now hardly control her voice.

"You see, Lili didn't come with me. She took me to an airplane in the middle of the night and then left me with a strange woman. I was so angry with her and so afraid.

"Later, I learned she tried one more time to save even more diamonds from the Nazi clutches and was caught and jailed at Breendonk concentration camp. But I thought she had abandoned me as well. Everyone had abandoned me. I felt like choking. I couldn't talk anymore. I just wanted to disappear myself."

Now Sarah turned to Madeleine, her adopted mother,

"I'm so sorry Mummy Madeleine for not accepting your and Daddy Gerald's love at first. You tried really everything to make me feel safe, while you yourself were so worried about not getting any message of Lili's whereabouts.

"And Rosalie also was so sweet to me, sharing her toys and her puddings. I just couldn't accept any of it. I was in such darkness, such pain. Only the piano was my solace. Thank you so much for buying me that grand piano and letting me play whenever I wanted. I must have driven you crazy with my scales and my terrible phase of atonal Dvorak. And never answering your questions."

Madeleine squeezed her daughter's hand, "Darling, there is nothing you should apologize for. Daddy and I were just very worried about you. And the doctors didn't know what was wrong with you - why you couldn't talk when there was physically nothing wrong with you. We had no clue who you were. You arrived with a small suitcase and a note saying we had to take care of you. We did the best we could and were very pleased to find out you enjoyed our battered old piano. It was immediately clear to us that you were very talented and needed a better piano. And look at you now. We couldn't be prouder and happier than having had the honor to raise you in our family. And the way you are able to talk about your very difficult past."

Sarah's eyes were now shimmering with tears, but she went on.

"Then Lili finally came back to England, but she was so thin and so ill. And she didn't know where my family was. But I loved her so much and when she told me she had saved the Goldmunz diamond, my father and my grandfather's prized diamond, I was just so grateful for all she had done for my family." Now Sarah faced the audience with her head high but tears streaming down her cheeks.

"My beloved grandfather, Isaac Goldmunz, died from his wounds in Fort Breendonk, only meters away from where Lili was held in her cell. Grandmama Elizabeth, and Great Aunt Agatha both died in Auschwitz. My father, Jacob, and my mother, Rachel, together with what would have been my little brother or sister, were killed in the gas chambers in Dachau. Mademoiselle Cohen died in Ravensbrück. I am the only survivor of the Goldmunz family, but I am a Hamilton too. I am both with all my heart.

"I know that my sister Lili Hamilton Brodie never seeks recognition for her actions – she simply did what needed to be done. Lili stops at nothing.

"But please see the impact of her deeds reflected in me. I am on my way to becoming a concert pianist. To make both my families proud. Without Lili, I would not even be alive today. Please, allow me to play for her, and for you all, the Prelude that I was practicing at the time. I know Chopin's Prelude in C Minor is a heavy piece, as it is also called the Funeral March, but that is – alas –a defining element of my life."

Sarah rose and bowed to the audience, then descended the few steps to the black grand piano that stood next to the orchestra pit. Madeleine reached out and squeezed Lili's hand, a silent gesture of solidarity and support.

Together, they watched as Sarah took her place at the piano, her fingers poised over the keys with a sense of quiet determination.

And then, as the first poignant notes of Chopin's Prelude in C Minor filled the air, clear and haunting, Lili closed her eyes and let the music wash over her, a balm for the soul, a reminder of the enduring power of hope and the unbreakable bonds of love that had brought them all together on this unforgettable evening.

The applause for Sarah, her words, and her music, was overpowering, filling the hall to the rafters.

In her quiet, lovely voice she said at last, "it is now my honor to present to you the next guest, Herr Hans Arenberg aka John.

22

THE GOOD GERMAN

The audience was still reeling from Sarah's harrowing account, when they saw her hand the microphone to a ruddy-faced man with short, blond hair and light-gray eyes.

No one outside Océane and Jean-Jacques knew who the tall man with the reserved, almost studious expression, was, not in the least that he was the German in their midst.

Hans Arenberg stood before the audience at Le Manoir, his hands clasped tightly around the microphone.

He glanced at Océane, his eyes reflecting a mix of gratitude and admiration, before turning his attention to the eager faces before him.

"*Bonjour à tous*," he began, his voice steady but tinged with emotion.

"It is truly an honor to be here today, to share with you the remarkable journey that brought me into the presence of one of the

bravest souls I've ever met and may now call my friend—Océane
Bell Riveau.

"I suppose you're all wondering who I am. A German, so much is
clear from my accent. I am well aware you may feel reserve, even
repulsion for me being on the same stage as a young survivor like
the young woman before me. You will be asking yourself what right
a German has, to show his face here when we've just heard what my
country did to Sarah's family. And you may even hate me when I tell
you I wore the *feldgrau* sergeant uniform of the Third Reich for a
couple of years."

Hans paused, taking a moment to gather his thoughts while
mopping the sweat from his forehead. He clearly struggled before
continuing, expecting the audience to rise as one and come after
him with pitchforks and scorn.

But nothing happened. The silence was careful, if a bit cold.

"Please let me explain before you judge me. I do apologize, on
behalf of Germany, for all that happened in the past two decades.
And I realize my apology is an empty echo in a bottomless pit of
pain and privation. But I want you to hold on to the sliver of hope
that there were Germans who had nothing with Nazidom, more
Germans than will ever step out of the shadows, both inside
Germany and in the armed forces.

"However, I wasn't invited here to give you a history lesson, or to
reduce the gravity of the war. I am also not here to ask for *your*
forgiveness. I ask forgiveness for my role in causing the sacrifices
these resistance women here on stage made to save their countries
and their people from the atrocities my people inflicted on them.

"It is my job to pray to my God every day and ask *His* forgiveness. He, who looks deeply into the heart of every soldier who took up the arms and did what we did. God will reckon with us in His way."

Hans's voice, with the clipped Germanic inflection carried the weight of memories long-held and pain deeply-buried.

"I was but a young soldier, no more than eighteen years old, reluctantly leaving my prosperous family estate near Hanover where I had a good life and no intention of ever leaving. I am a farmer's son and farming is my blood and soul. But, alas, my tranquil Junker's life was brutally uprooted when I was forced to serve under a commander whose character I soon came to question."

Hans hesitated, sought Océane's eyes. She gave him a reassuring nod.

"After France surrendered to Germany, I was stationed in Paris, a huge city, which was nothing but a confusing madhouse to me after never having left the rural quiet of our estate. I was homesick, dumbstruck, intimidated. I fell ill."

Hans's gaze drifted to Océane again. Now a wan smile graced his lips as he addressed her directly.

"Doctor Bell and my path first crossed during those early days of the war in Paris.

"I still feel it as if fate intervened, leading me to her capable physician's hands in the hospital Hôtel-Dieu. She immediately saw that my shortness of breath was not my battling with chest ailments that plagued me, but the inner turmoil of my soul caught in the

throes of war. I can tell you...," now Hans's gaze wandered to
Capitaine Heurtier,

"...that a wounded soldier, whether physically wounded or mentally
exhausted, who encounters a compassionate doctor feels like he's
been saved from entering through the doors of Hell."

Gratitude shone in the depths of Hans's eyes as he addressed
both mother and daughter, the two physicians on stage.

"Though Océane, who at the time was *Madame Docteur* to me of
course, saw the uniform I wore, she saw beyond it, beyond the
façade of duty I was still clinging to. She saw my fear, my doubt, the
humanity that lay beneath, and she offered me her help, without
judgment or reservation. She also instantly understood the complex
relationship between General von Stein, my commander, and me.
As Von Stein had been her patient in the same hospital only weeks
earlier, she understood my fear."

Hans paused, his chest swelling with emotion.

"Some people are evil. Maybe they're not born evil but based on
what they've gone through in life they make the wrong choices and
become depraved, sick souls. Von Stein was one of those people
and yes, alas, we had plenty of those serving under the Nazi
regime.

"But let us focus on the good. With Océane's help, I found solace,
strength, and a renewed sense of purpose. She reminded me that
even amid a war that wasn't mine but that I couldn't escape – at least
not at the time - there existed moments of compassion, of kindness,
of hope. Little did I know how intricately her life and mine would

become interwoven until we were even brothers in arms, so to speak."

Hans turned to face the audience, his gaze alight with reverence for *his* Madame Docteur. Next, he took a deep breath, searching for words, the weight of the past again heavy on his shoulders.

"I was but a young sergeant, stationed at 84 Avenue Foch, the headquarters of the French Gestapo in Paris, in the clutches of a man I despised as much as feared - General Von Stein. Can you imagine my surprise when one day, as I was posted at the front door, I see Madame Docteur come up the stairs as if she hasn't a care in the world?

"Of course, I wondered what was going on when she asked me to take her to Von Stein's office. During my visit to Hôtel Dieu Hospital, she'd told me that Von Stein had also been there in her care, so I assumed she'd come to the hellhole of occupied Paris in her role as physician.
"You see, as most French know but maybe non-French don't, during the war 84 Avenue Foch was the place where resistance fighters were taken to be interrogated and tortured. Every day I heard the screams from the top floors and regularly one of these desperate prisoners would jump out of a window, usually to their death. Very few managed to escape."

Hans rubbed a hand over his eyes as if trying to wipe away the horrible recollections.

"Anyway, sorry, I'm digressing. It wasn't my business to know what Docteur Océane Bell was doing in my part of the underworld, but I was sure glad to see her kind, smiling face as she recognized me.

"As I came to find out, Océane was there on a mission of her own. Her beloved Jean-Jacques Riveau was missing, and as he was with the French Resistance, she gathered he'd probably been taken to 84 Avenue Foch."

"So, she risked her own life to uncover the truth, to find he who meant everything to her, her now-husband, the father of her twin boys, Max and Bertrand."

Hans's gray eyes went from Océane to Jean-Jacques who was sitting front row with tears in his eyes. The Frenchman saluted Hans as a way of thanking him for the heart-warming tribute to his wife. Hans continued, his voice thick with the emotions of the past.

"Driven by desperation and determination, Océane dared to confront Von Stein, the man who held sway over the lives of his prisoners. I later found out she feigned concern for his failing health, a guise of compassion to mask her true intentions. But Von Stein, as ever the master manipulator, saw through her cover-up, yet chose to keep her close, to use her as his so-called personal physician."

As he spoke, the audience leaned in closer, captivated by the tale of courage and sacrifice unfolding before them.

"Now we were both, possibly all three, in Von Stein's power, but the whereabouts of Jean-Jacques, codenamed Remix, remained unclear. And then, by a sudden change of fate, Océane and I found ourselves together with Von Stein in Libya, the unforgiving desert sands of North Africa stretching out before us. Somehow Von Stein had been reposted there and I joined as his chauffeur and Océane as his doctor.

"It was there, in the blistering heat and swirling sands, that she discovered the truth of my allegiance, my true desire to break free from the shackles of war and the unhealthy relationship Von Stein had forced me into. You see…," Hans hesitated, swallowed hard, "Von Stein not only owned me as a soldier, he owned me in all possible ways. I was no more than a slave."

For a moment he hung his head in shame but soon looked up with more fervour in the gray eyes.

"Von Stein had severe heart problems and because of all the medication he took, he was far from clear-headed and also had terrible bouts of anger. Océane and I started plotting our escape, which we thought could be successful in such an unforgiving and deserted place.

"But then the Allies, our friends unbeknownst to them, began a counterattack and we had to bring Von Stein into hiding in an underground bunker in the middle of the desert. He was delirious by that time and… and we took our chance with him. We had no other choice. It was his life, or ours." Hans's gaze locked with Océane, and the memory of those harrowing hours and their decision was palpable across the expanse of the hall.

"We fled as soon as it was dark, no lights on the Kubelwagen, until we found refuge with a division of the First Free French led by the incredible Thierry Duval at an oasis in the Allied territory. After some initial mistrust, our loyalties became clear. And what is most amazing of all…," Hans now directly addressed the audience, "… unknown to Océane, Jean-Jacques, who'd managed to flee France, was at the oasis in North Africa as well, now under the codename Huricana. He couldn't blow his cover, but he later told his beloved that his heart broke not being able to step out of the shadows and let her know he was alive. At the time the 'cause' was still the most important to hide his cover.

"We were helped back into France, and we both joined the French Resistance, I as Jean and Océane as The Rose. But we only met again at the end of the war, sitting side by side near the Seine and talking about our lives since the last time we met and about our lives before the war. I will always remember that Seine talk as one of the most important meetings of my life. We shared our deepest secrets and pains with each other.

"I told Océane about my own Anna, a wonderful girl who'd stood up against Nazidom from within Germany back in 1933. I hadn't heard from her in years. Didn't even know if she was still alive, as she was an active member of the White Roses, the Resistance movement inside Germany.

"It is my pleasure to tell you all that Anna and I were able to find each other back in the ruins of post-war Germany and that she's even here with me today at Le Manoir. We are happily married and parents to the wonderful Cece. Her name a tribute to the woman who saved my soul, my life, my future."

His eyes filling with tears, his voice hoarse, he concluded,

"Océane, my dear, dear friend, you have been a beacon of hope to me in the darkest of times. Together with you, I dared to forge a path to redemption, leaving behind the shadows of my past to embrace a future filled with promise and possibility. I am eternally thankful to you. May God bless you and your beautiful family."

As his words echoed through the hall, a silent acknowledgment passed between the two friends, a testament to the bond that had carried them through the trials of war and into the light of a new day.

Océane grabbed his hand, which Hans brought to his mouth and kissed.

"And with this, my tribute to Océane Bell-Riveau ends. I hand the microphone to a young lady with an extraordinary story of love and survival, Rebecca Weiss."

23

AS IT HAD LIVED BEFORE

With a graceful bow, a slender woman with chestnut-brown eyes and an oval face rose and took the microphone from Hans, who was now affectionately known as "the good German."

"Thank you, Hans," she began, her gaze sweeping over the assembled audience. Though older than Sarah Goldmunz-Hamilton, there was a shared sorrow evident in their eyes, a reflection of lives scarred by loss and grief.

"I am Rebecca Weiss, Esther's younger sister, three years her junior," Rebecca announced in her melodious voice. "Together, we are the sole survivors of the Weiss family of Vienna. I sit here at Le Manoir, not only as a tribute to my incredible sister Esther, but also in memory of our beloved parents, Franz and Naomi Weiss, our younger brother Adam, and our Aunt Isobel Gjelsvik Weiss, all of whom perished in the hellish depths of German concentration camps.

"While Esther valiantly fought in the Norwegian Resistance together with her now-husband Tore Helberg, I was in Auschwitz and Ravensbrück, which I survived, miracle of miracles."

As she spoke, Rebecca's features tightened, showing her immeasurable pain and her voice, though clear, trembled as she continued.

"Before I tell you about the horrors of war and how Esther helped to restore my shattered spirit, allow me to give you an idea of the Weiss family before the war and before all we knew was darkness and pain."

Pausing to collect herself, Rebecca drew a shaky breath, her expression haunted by the memories of a stolen childhood. But her voice was soft with nostalgia when she painted the picture of the more idyllic part of their lives in Vienna.

"We, the Weiss children – Esther, Adam, and myself – were fortunate to experience a childhood filled with laughter and adventure in the beautiful capital of Austria, Vienna. Our winter holidays were spent skiing in the majestic Austrian Alps, while summers were marked by city excursions to London, Amsterdam, and Rome, exploring the wonders of Europe.

"Our father was an esteemed Viennese jeweler and had a spacious shop and atelier on Prater Strasse, a center of craftsmanship and elegance in the heart of Vienna. Our family lived in a spacious apartment over the shop, and our grandmother, whom we called Oma, lived with us.
Our father's dedication to his craft, which he had learned from his father, earned him the respect of the community, both Jewish and

non-Jewish. Our Mutti and Oma regaled us with tales of tea parties and grand balls attended by Vienna's elite."

Rebecca's voice was tinged with a longing for those days of innocence. Esther grabbed her sister's hand and squeezed it softly, while her other hand rested on her growing belly.

Her eyes were moist, but she sat regal and tall as ever. All ears for her beloved sister, her only surviving family. After a quick glance shared between sisters, Rebecca carried on.

"Even before her eighteenth birthday at the beginning of 1938, Esther was already betrothed to the son of another respected Viennese goldsmith family, the Bernsteins. So yes, we had a comfortable and happy life despite the anti-Jewish sentiments that followed Hitler's chancellorship in 1933.

"Well, our lovely life didn't last. And we never saw it coming, blindly hoping Austria would stay independent from Germany. But a black cloud descended over the Austrians in March 1938, when the annexation became a reality. Without putting up even the pretense of protest, the Austrian government surrendered to the German Reich. The annexation altered the course of our lives, and of all Austrian Jews, irrevocably."

Rebecca's narrative was captivating, now drawing the audience into the tale of her family's journey from Vienna to Norway.

"Imagine Vienna, once vibrant and full of life, and full of Jews," Rebecca's warm smile broke over her face showing she had once upon a time been a vivacious and fun-loving being. "But that soon changed under the growing National Socialist influence after the annexation.

"Esther, at the time still the dreamer and schemer she'd always been, envisioned a grand Viennese wedding where the two jeweler families, the Weisses and the Bernsteins, would finally join together. So, off she went to Le Manoir, though she was a more than accomplished housewife already, but Esther never went for anything less than perfection."

Esther laughed out loud at the way her sister poked fun of her ideal life. How different everything had gone.

Rebecca continued unperturbed, clearly feeling more at ease in her role as one of the speakers.

"After Kristallnacht, our father made the difficult decision to move the family including old Oma, to Oslo, where his sister, our Aunt Isobel and her husband Frerik lived. Esther was still here in Switzerland, but would join us later.

"We left behind our old life, hoping for peace in a new land. The Hoffmans, Asher and his family, had already moved to Holland.

"So, we found ourselves in Norway, a country that was very different from Austria, where we'd always lived. But though it was colder, and the food always tasted of fish and the language sounded as if they were perpetually cheerful, Oslo and the Gjelsvik family became our sanctuary. We traded opulence for coziness and adjusted as best as we could."

Rebecca sought Tore's face in the front row. "

Especially my friendship with Tore Helberg meant a lot to me. He and his family next door were so kind. Tore was a student at the time, but he never felt it beneath him to play the guitar for me when

I came to him, lugging my violin case behind me. And Bodil, their dog, was so sweet. They made Norway feel like home to me.

"However, not everything was smooth sailing when Esther joined us. I mean between Esther and Tore. Let's just say Esther hated him with a vengeance," Rebecca giggled amused. "A spilled cup of cocoa on her engagement day in the Austrian Alps was the cause. Too long of a story to share now, but one that will be told around the fireplace until these two have reached old age.

"Imagine our shock when Hitler also invaded Norway. At first, we dismissed the significance of the German occupation and held on to a false sense of security because our new country was so big. It would certainly shield us from the horrors the Jews suffered in Austria.

"We retreated to a farmstead in the countryside, just to be sure. We lived in a small house on the farmstead of Tore's grandparents, the Lindenbergs. With Oma becoming frailer by the day, we needed to be away from the cramped Gjelsvik apartment in the capital where the German presence was everywhere."

Rebecca stopped for a moment, looked at her sister, who nodded back. *Go on tell everything. I'm here.*

"But then, an unwelcome visitor shattered our fragile peace. He was Norwegian but he kept asking questions. *Who we were. Where we were from.* Despite our suspicions, we didn't want to think of fleeing again.

"Esther, with her blond hair and light eyes resembled the locals, so she did all our shopping and Oma was being looked after on the Lindenberg farm.

"Our illusion of safety was shattered when the Germans came for us. That Norwegian was a Quisling - he worked for the Germans." Rebecca's voice trembled at the memory. "We were stripped of our belongings and our freedom, forced onto a truck bound for an unknown fate. Mutti, Vati, Adam, and I.

"Adam, who was only fourteen, was so afraid. Though it was warm in June, his teeth kept clattering and he needed a warm pullover while he was also sweating, as if he had a fever. But Mutti and Vati were strong and spoke soft words to us to keep us anchored in hope.

"Our arrest had gone so fast we'd only had time to pack the most essentials things. I wanted so much to leave a note for Esther, but the Germans wouldn't let me. Not being able to say goodbye to Esther haunted me from that day forward, every day, day-in and day-out, from one camp to the next. The agony I knew our sudden and seemingly secret departure must have caused her tormented me until... until we met again after the war."

REBECCA SPED UP HER TALKING, as if wanting to have it over and done with.

"The truck that was loaded with Norwegian Jews took us through southern Norway and then into Denmark. Mutti with her foresight had quickly packed as some extra clothes and food for the journey. But there was no toilet and the truck only stopped for short moments."

Her tone now became measured and reflective.

"But, my dear friends, there are chapters of our lives that we dare not revisit, places so dark that even the bravest souls tremble at the mere thought.

"In preparing for this evening, I sought counsel from my therapist. He advised against delving too deeply into my time in the camps, urging me instead to focus on the light that guides us forward.

"Tonight, I am here before you not as a survivor of Auschwitz and Ravensbrück, but as a tribute to the unyielding courage of my sister Esther. My presence here is a celebration of life, of Esther's search to find me... to find her family after her own ordeal.

"For four long years, she fought alongside the brave souls of the Norwegian Resistance, defying tyranny and oppression at every turn. She helped her adopted country fight its way back to freedom and she did everything... literally everything, to make that come to pass. Even after she was arrested by the Gestapo herself and miraculously escaped with the help of Tore.

"All I will say about my years in the camps is that agony and despair were our constant companions and tragedy struck with unfathomable frequency and cruelty. On arrival in Auschwitz, Mutti and I were separated at the station from Vati and Adam, so we faced the grim reality of our existence with the family further fractured.

"We had never lived like that before. Vati had made all the important decisions in our life. I know that may sound old-fashioned, but it was the reality in our household. Not that Mutti and Oma were weak women, but fending for ourselves without Vati was a new situation.

"I did everything in my power to make my mother as comfortable as possible, but she grew weaker and weaker with the hard work we had to perform and the little food we were given. Soon after we arrived in Ravensbrück she passed..."

Rebecca's voice was barely audible as she whispered in the microphone.

"To be honest it was a strange sort of relief to see her suffering finally ended, but missing Mutti was unbearable. I lived in a black hole.

"Only after the war I learned our beloved brother Adam was sent straight to the gas chambers and Vati worked on the construction of roads until he too perished. Aunt Isobel, who was later arrested in Oslo, and Esther's fiancé Carl also didn't survive.

"For me it would have been a matter of days, when the Americans came to our liberation. I don't think I would have survived another week. I was in hospital for a long, long time..." Her voice trailed off.

"But never underestimate Esther Weiss Helberg. She found me. She came and nursed me back to life. She came and is, and always will be, my everything, my big sister, my example, my savior."

Tears streamed down Rebecca's cheeks, but her eyes also glistened with joy.

"Esther's solace in her years of loneliness was a book her friend

Anna gave her, *Rebecca* by Daphne du Maurier. She told me many
times that only reading a few sentences in the book helped her
believe I was still around somewhere.

"This quote in particular: *'As I stood there, hushed and still, I could
swear that the house was not an empty shell but lived and breathed as it
had lived before.'*

"And now Esther and Tore have set up the Franz and Naomi Weiss
Recuperation Center near Oslo and they have built a new house
that is full of life and hope. And I could not be happier to be part of
it, though I am away sometimes as I study music theory at Oslo
University."

Rebecca's eyes now grew even brighter, and she rose from her
chair.

"I have a final announcement to make before I hand the
microphone to the next esteemed guest. I would like to introduce to
you a new member of the Weiss family. We've kept this even secret
from Esther and Tore...

"Tonight, I announce my upcoming engagement to the wonderful
and very handsome Mr. Ben Adler. He is a renowned Jewish-
Norwegian poet and also a concentration camp survivor. But, first
and foremost, he is my soulmate."

A tall, slender man with curly black hair and gold-rimmed spec-
tacles on his thin nose rose from his chair in the second row and
bowed left and right to the public.

"I love you too, my pretty princess!" he called to Rebecca and
blew her a kiss.

Esther had risen too and was hugging her sister wildly.

"Oh, my goodness, what a delight! A baby and a wedding! I couldn't be happier."

The sisters kissed cheeks before Rebecca spoke her final words. "Tonight, we honor not only the lives lost but also the ones saved, the bonds forged in adversity, and the triumph of the human spirit. It is, therefore, my greatest honor to hand the microphone to our next guest, Mr Freddie Frinton-Smith."

24

MORE THAN FRIENDS

A man in a blue RAF suit, his chest heavily hung with decorations, accepted the microphone from Rebecca with a gracious smile. He had slick black hair and blue eyes.

He was a slender man, a graceful man, who clearly took up his position in the world with unbridled confidence. But what struck the audience most was his similarity to the woman next to him, Sable Montgomery Mitchell.

Aware of the surprised looks he was receiving and always the showman, Freddie immediately burst forward with the truth.

"Ah, I daresay you've all noticed the uncanny resemblance between myself and the exquisite beauty gracing my side. Indeed, officially, I go by the moniker Freddie Frinton-Smith – yes, yes, from the whiskey brand – though in truth, I am but Freddo, and this delightful creature is none other than my beloved half-sister, Sabbo.

"We hail from neighboring estates amidst the rugged splendor of the Scottish Highlands, yet our familial ties clearly run deeper than mere geography. We share the same mother, though it took a chance encounter amidst the tumult of wartime France to uncover that truth.

"Clearly, we were destined more for kinship than conjugal bliss." Freddie laughed out loud, giving Sable a wink. "Remember our ill-fated attempt at secret wedding, sis? Ah, well, such is life.! "Fortunately Sabbo found her match in the dashing Wild Bill while I, as you can plainly see,"

he quipped, tracing a playful arc around his visage with a lopsided grin,

"would hardly have passed muster in that role.
"So, here's to David Southgate, my steadfast comrade-in-arms for nigh on fifteen years. His unwavering patience surely merits a round of applause for enduring my antics. But let us not forget Wild Bill, who undoubtedly deserves all commendation for taming Sabbo. Or, perhaps it was the other way around. I wasn't present to ascertain the precise details."

"It was Daddy who tamed Mummy, Uncle Freddie." Isabella's high-pitched giggle sounded from the audience. Freddie tapped his absent cap in a mock salute. "There you go, Bella my dear, it's one-nil to the men."

The audience laughed, much in need of some light banter after the heavy, emotional stories they'd heard. And Freddie had a magnetic personality that drew in anyone listening.

His Oxford brogue, the elegant waving of his arms, and his lively personality were as irresistible as the force of gravity, but through it all, his charm conveyed a deep love and respect for his sister.

"Sabbo saved my life. Not once, but twice. Let me first regale you with a tale of misadventure and daring escapades amidst the tumult of the start of the war in Europe. Picture this: a clear, blue sky marred by the ominous drone of enemy aircraft, our aircraft, a Lysander, and thus a fine specimen of British engineering, was sent hurtling to the earth in a chaotic cacophony of twisted metal and billowing smoke. Yes, my dear friends, David and I found ourselves plummeting from the heavens, our fate dangling precariously in the balance when landing on Belgium soil.

"And our fall was not without its perils. David, poor chap, suffered a severe head injury during the fall, leaving him incapacitated and at the mercy of enemy fire. Oh, the horror of it all! The deafening roar of German guns, the acrid stench of burning wreckage, the relentless barrage from above and below. Hundreds of thousands of Belgians and British and French soldiers fleeing south, to the coast. To the beaches of Dunkirk. And all the while, the sun shone, and the birds tried to chirp.

"Yet, amidst the chaos, when we were on that strip of sand and could go no farther, a glimmer of hope emerged on the horizon. Behold, the miraculous sight of vessels, stalwart and resolute, making their valiant approach across the Channel. With my last strength, I plunged into the frigid waters, bearing David's unconscious form upon my shoulders, each step forward a stroke of luck and a prayer for survival.

"Boats sank around us like dominoes, brave souls left and right succumbed to the merciless embrace of the sea. Yet, against all odds, salvation beckoned from the deck of a vessel, where none other than Sable herself extended a lifeline to David and me in our hour of need. Oh, the irony of it all! The unlikely savior, plucking us from the jaws of despair with a flourish worthy of a Shakespearean drama."

Though Freddie never stopped smiling and pulled out all the stops to entertain the audience, his blue eyes were serious and his hand, with a glittering diamond ring on his pinkie, resting on Sable's sleeve quivered.

His voice dropped an octave as he continued.

"I am before you today, a survivor of Dunkirk's harrowing trials. Thanks to The Canterbury, Captain Hancock, and Sable, David and I were among the lucky devils who safely reached Dover and could continue to fight in the war. Though, my dear David, bless his cotton socks, certainly took his sweet time recuperating from his little rendezvous with Belgian terra firma.

"Let me now tell you about the second time Sable rescued me, or rather we rescued each other but I couldn't have done it without her. Sabbo and I, ever the intrepid souls, answered the call to duty by enlisting in the Special Operations Executive to become secret agents. With her indomitable spirit, she ventured forth first, joining the Chassis Network in Lyon. But when German infiltration threatened her cover, she pivoted her efforts to the Bordeaux region, unaware of my impending arrival within the Papillon Network.

"Imagine my astonishment when, on a moonlit night, I found myself descending from yet another Lysander aircraft, only to discover my dear friend Sabbo waiting for me below. Oh, the joy of our reunion, tempered only by the strict protocols of secrecy that governed our clandestine operations.

"But amidst the hushed exchanges and covert gestures, Sabbo revealed a startling revelation: our mother, may her serpentine soul rest in peace, had recently departed this world in Monte Carlo. And amid her affairs, she left behind a missive that unraveled a familial secret of seismic proportions – an illicit liaison between my father and her, resulting in my own humble existence. Quite the twist, wouldn't you agree?"

The smile temporarily became a shadow, but Freddie regained control and carried on.

"Indeed, it was a revelation of sorts, discovering that Sabbo and I shared a blood connection that just added to the sense of familial bond we had always shared. Despite the initial shock of our newfound connection, we found solace and strength in our shared experiences and aspirations. Our partnership flourished amidst the trials of wartime espionage, our minds attuned to the same frequency of daring and determination.

"Yet, as fate would have it, our unity was tested by the cruel hand of betrayal. A mole had infiltrated our network, and so we found ourselves ensnared in the clutches of the Gestapo, our lives hanging by a thread.

"But even in the face of adversity, we refused to yield. With steely resolve, we seized upon the one fleeting opportunity we had for escape. Together, we chiseled away for hours at the bars of our prison, finally forging a path to freedom. And though it may sound cliché, I must confess, I owe my liberty and my life to none other than my dear sister."

"Oh, we did it together, Freddo. Really!" Sable exclaimed.

"Ah no. You swooped in and handled Henri De Bonheur with such finesse, the traitor never took another breath and would not have a chance to double-cross another agent. I, on the other hand, made a strategic retreat as swiftly as my legs could propel me."

Freddie beamed with pride, his admiration for her shining brightly in his eyes.

"True, but it was a sordid affair. I'm glad you weren't there," Sable mumbled, "now tell them you saved me as well."

"If I must, I will. But it was really a trivial affair, compared to all you did for me and for David. But alright, ladies and gentlemen, let me beat my own drum then for a moment if I may.

"When our dear Sabbo found herself weary from the rigors of her covert missions in France, who do you think was there to tend to her, to nurse her back to health with all the care and tenderness in the world? Yours truly, of course!

"And after the war, when the shadows of the past still lingered, it was my great privilege to aid Sable in her quest to reunite with her daughter, Isabella, who'd been given up for adoption at birth.

"Ah, there's nothing I wouldn't do for my dear sister Sable, and let it be known far and wide that her bravery as a secret agent knew no bounds. The Raven was a force to be reckoned with, a true heroine of the Allied cause, instrumental in the success of the D-Day landings. So let us raise our glasses and give three resounding cheers for the unequaled Sable Montgomery-Mitchell!"

"Mummy, Mummy, Mummy!" Isabella shrieked over everyone else. The cheering went on for a long time until the calm returned, and Freddie picked up the microphone for the final time.

"Ladies and gentlemen, it is my distinct pleasure to introduce our next speaker, none other than the esteemed Dutchman Mr. Jan Meulenbelt, affectionately known to Edda as Ome Jan..."

25

AN EYE FOR AN EYE

O me Jan was a man of stout posture with six decades of
life etched upon his weathered face. He used to sling
crates down by the Amsterdam docks, but when the
Germans marched in, he traded his work boots for resistance boots
in a heartbeat.

A black patch hid one of his eyes, a grim souvenir from the harsh
interrogations by the Gestapo. Yet, despite the scars of his trials, his
spirit remained unyielding, his presence commanding respect.

His attire spoke to his humble origins. But inside his rough exterior beat the heart of a lion.

Jan Meulenbelt was not just a man; he was a force of nature. And
his devotion to Edda rivaled that of his own kin.

Jan grabbed the microphone Freddie passed to him, eyeing the
thing as if it were some odd contraption from a different planet. But
then, he shrugged off his skepticism and began to speak into it all
the same.

"Alright, folks, gather round. Let me tell you a tale that starts with a lassie named Edda, a proper blue-blooded ballerina, mind you. Now, how did I, Jan Meulenbelt, a simple dockworker from Amsterdam, end up tangled in her world, you may wonder?

"Well, it all began when me sister Riet, bless her memory, lived next door to Edda in the Vondelstraat. From the get-go of the war, me sister was dropping hints to Edda that she wasn't too keen on them bloomin' Germans occupying our streets. You see, the Meulenbelts, we've been socialists since the dawn of time, and we've had a fair share of run-ins with Nazis.

"Me eyes were opened wide when I saw what they did to the Jewish folk who worked alongside me down at the docks. It was downright appalling, I tell ya. And it wasn't just me, the whole lot of us knew we had to stand up and fight against this injustice. Sure, me missus Christina, bless her heart, was fretting over the risks, but there was no doubt in me bones – I had to join the Resistance.

"So, I lent me hand in organizing the February Strikes of 1941, the only bit of open resistance against the persecution of Jews in all of Europe. But let me tell ya, mates, it didn't do Amsterdam or our Dutch Jews any good. Over 80% of 'em never made it back from them blasted concentration camps."

Jan fished out a sizable red and white handkerchief from his pocket, mopping his broad forehead with a hefty swipe. His lone functional eye sought out Edda beside him, and one couldn't help but notice the striking contrast between the two.

Here sat the burly, weathered man, with his flushed face and somewhat awkward demeanor, while next to him Edda sat as the poised and graceful ballerina, her elegance evident to all present. But the bond between them transcended all societal differences.

"Well, you see, my dear sister Riet always was the nosy type, being an early widow without children of herself. But in this case, her snooping proved to be a blessing. You see, Edda's parents, they were prominent NSB-ers. Yeah, those Nazi sympathizers. And to make matters worse for her own safety, Edda was cozying up with a Jewish lad. Talk about trouble brewing, eh?

"Riet, bless her soul, she's got this knack for sniffing out trouble like a bloodhound on a scent. So, when she got wind of Edda's situation, she wasted no time in raising the alarm. And let me tell you, when Riet raised the alarm, you listened.

"Anyway, she reckoned that Edda might be in double danger on account of her parents' associations and her... shall we say, forbidden romance. And you know what? She was right. Bloody Nazis. Always causing trouble, they were. But we weren't about to let them have their way, not on our watch.

"Riet could tell Edda wanted to steer clear of her Nazi-sympathizing parents, and who could blame her, really? No one wants to be tangled up with that lot. And poor Edda, she was caught between a rock and a hard place, with no family to turn to.

"It's a sorry state of affairs when your own flesh and blood are on the wrong side of history. But let me tell you, Riet, she had a heart of gold, that woman. She took Edda under her wing like a mother hen, she did. Made sure she had a safe place to lay her head at night, away from all that Nazi nonsense.

"And I reckon Edda was grateful for it, even if she didn't always show it. Sometimes family ain't about blood, you know? It's about who's got your back when the chips are down. And Tante Riet, she had Edda's back, through thick and thin. And the other way around."

Jan paused, mopping his forehead again. His one good eye showing despair.

"Well, you might be thinking, 'What did us lot in the Dutch Resistance really do?' Simple, really. We did what we could to keep them Nazis from getting their hands on folks they shouldn't. We hid away Jews, sure, but not just them. Anyone the Nazis had it out for, really. Communists, too. We'd find 'em a safe place to lay low until the coast was clear. It weren't glamorous work, mind you, but it was necessary. Someone had to stand up to those buggers, and if it wasn't gonna be us, then who?

"So, one day, it was sometime in July 1943, I was minding me own business at the dock, when out of the blue, I'm surrounded by those bloody Gestapo agents. Talk about a surprise party, eh? They dragged me off to their headquarters on the Elandgracht, where they put me through the wringer, I tell ya. Punch after punch, blow after blow, but old Jan here wasn't about to spill the beans. No names, no safe houses, no networks. They could torture me all they wanted, but I wasn't giving 'em an inch.

"Now, I'm not one to exaggerate, but things were looking pretty grim. I was expecting them to cart me off to the dunes for a one-way ticket to the afterlife. Not that I was too bothered by the idea at the time, mind you. I was a right bloody mess, hurting like you wouldn't believe.

"Can't say I remember much of what happened next, seeing as I was out cold for most of it. But there was a bit of a ruckus, shots ringing out and whatnot, and then, out of nowhere, I find meself being carried off by none other than Edda here and another lad from the Resistance we called Rick. Now, Rick was training to be a doctor, and somehow, they managed to get me to a safehouse in Haarlem. And that, my friends, is how I survived, though I did lose an eye to the interrogation.

"So, I suppose you're all itching to know how Edda got wind that the Gestapo had it in for me, right? Well, it's a bit of a tale. You see, my missus, Christina, caught wind that I'd been nabbed for questioning. Quick as a flash, she dashed off to my sister Riet's place and spilled the beans. And Riet, being the smart cookie she was, wasted no time in getting word to Edda.

"Now, Edda and that young bloke Rick knew that if the Nazis got hold of me and squeezed me dry, the whole Amsterdam Resistance would come crashing down like a house of cards. I knew too much, you see.

"So, they set up shop near the police station, keeping their eyes peeled until they spotted me being bundled into that blasted Kubelwagen. Without skipping a beat, they hopped on the back and tagged along for the fifteen-kilometer jaunt to the dunes.

"Once we arrived, they sprang into action, catching the Germans off guard and giving 'em what-for. And let me tell you, folks, that wasn't just any ol' rescue mission; it was a downright miracle.

"Edda not only saved my skin that day, but she saved my bloomin' soul. And for that, I'll be forever in her debt."

The one good eye spilled a tear as it took in the sight of Edda. The voice grew softer as Jan continued.

"Well, I have to tell you, folks, there were some dark days during that summer of '44, when that wretched Klaas Bollema, that traitorous snake of an NSB storm trooper, sold out Riet and Edda to the Gestapo. It felt like a punch straight to the gut. That slimy traitor was none other than Edda's old man's former driver. Bollema handed 'em over to the enemy, but in the process, Edda made sure he'd never live to tell the tale.

"Me sister and Edda, they were taken away, carted off to Camp Westerbork. But let me tell you something about Tante Riet - she was me right-hand woman in the Resistance. The Gestapo knew that, oh, they knew it alright. So, I had to lay low, keep moving from one safe house to the next, dodging them like a cat dodges raindrops. But when the liberation finally came, we learned it had come too late for Riet. They'd put her in front of a firing squad, just like that.

"Edda, bless her heart, was spared that fate, but she endured her own hell in that camp. And let me tell you, folks, the loss of me sister, it still hits me like a ton of bricks. But Edda, she's like a daughter to me now, and her pain is me pain. We're in this together, through thick and thin.

"Now, I was saved, but... it was like having one foot in the grave and the other in a pit of despair, ya know? The thrill of making it out alive is there, sure, but it's now forever shadowed over by her loss. Riet Meulenberg, she was a real firecracker, and I'm damn proud she was me sister.

"Now, this feisty lady next to me, me Edda or 'kindje' as Riet used to call her, she's also a true force of nature. Apart from saving me sorry hide, she rescued countless Jews, whisking them away to safety in the countryside. And let me tell you, I'll be forever indebted to her and her sweetheart, Ash Hoffman, who miraculously survived those hellish concentration camps. They're married now, with a little one of their own.

"Damn the Nazis! We fought 'em tooth and nail for a free Holland."

Jan raised his fist triumphantly before rising to plant kisses on both of Edda's cheeks. She practically disappeared in his bear hug.

Then, turning to address the audience, Jan introduced the final speaker, "now, I've got the pleasure of passing the microphone over to that English lassie, Pearl Baseden. Good luck to you, girl."

26

WHAT SHE STOOD FOR

As Dutch Jan finished his impassioned speech, Pearl Baseden Southgate rose from her seat, her small frame cutting a determined figure against the backdrop of the dark, Le Manoir curtains on stage.

With a confident air, she held the microphone between slender fingers, her short, dark-blonde hair framing her face like a halo, her sparkling eyes reflecting both resilience and somberness.

The pronounced, dark eyebrows furrowed slightly under the weight of her upcoming speech.

In the hall, where the air was thick with the collective emotion of the preceding speeches, anticipation hung palpably as Pearl prepared to share her own tale in the tributes to the Resistance Girls.

The audience leaned in, eager to hear the final chapter of bravery and sacrifice.

Turning to Anna Adams, her best friend and the one who'd sent her on her perilous mission as a SOE agent into France, Pearl's expression softened with gratitude and acknowledgment.

Her eyes gleamed with determination, while her voice carried a hint of her French heritage.

"*Merci*, Ome Jan, if I may call you that too? Thank you for that heartfelt introduction. And to all of you, *Mesdames et Messieurs*, for your patient ears listening to our shared tales of valor and resilience tonight. I suspect your ears may be buzzing with all you have heard, yet here I stand, ready to share my own trials and tribulations."

Pearl's voice, though resolute, carried a hint of vulnerability beneath her steadfast demeanor.

"You see, I simply couldn't remain seated when speaking of her. Not when it comes to Anna, my dear friend and savior. *Non, non!* Standing seems the only fitting tribute for one who always stood so tall, even if she remained in the shadows.

"I, Pearl Baseden Southgate, stand before you not merely as a survivor of the Third Reich horrors, but as a testament to the unbreakable courage of all resisters who dared to defy tyranny. And Anna was one of those. Every day of the war."

There was such fierce pride in Pearl's voice that all eyes went to Anna, who pushed her glasses up her nose and seemed to blush.

"It was Flight Officer Anna Adams, our spymaker from SOE Section France, who never ceased to search for us, her missing agents, long after the guns fell silent, and the world moved on.

"Contrary to the men in uniform who ran the Baker Street Headquarters in London, Anna, with her boundless determination and compassion, refused to accept us as mere casualties of conflict."

PEARL'S VOICE WAVERED SLIGHTLY, betraying the weight of gratitude she carried for Anna's relentless pursuit of justice.

"Mind you, Anna was never just a figurehead behind a London desk; she was the heart and soul of our missions to France, the fierce protector of our band of daring souls, men *and* women, who danced with danger in the shadows of war.

"Anna was never just content to sit idly by while her agents ventured into the belly of the beast. No, she was in the Signals Room night and day to wait for messages from the field, kept in touch with our family and friends and knew all our circumstances, our Networks, our roles ... and our weaknesses. For which she feared like no other, knowing how good the Germans were at tracking down her vulnerable agents who often operated solo.

"I am sure Anna had, long before the war ended, decided she would charge headfirst into the aftermath to ensure no agent disappeared without a trace nor a set of well-deserved medals, posthumous if necessary.

"While the military men might have seen us as mere pawns on a chessboard, Anna saw us as comrades, as friends, as family. She knew each of us by name, by heart, and by soul. Fifteen missing female agents and eighty-five male agents weren't just a number to Anna; we were one-hundred pieces of her heart lost to the cruel whims of fate.

"With her trademark gusto and silent passion, Anna left no stone unturned, no lead unchecked, in her relentless quest to bring her lost sheep back into the fold. And it was through her dogged determination that she unearthed me, languishing in the shadows of a forgotten hospital in Odessa."

With a resolute nod, Pearl's gaze swept across the room, her voice resonating with the echoes of those who had fought and fallen beside her.

"So, permit me a moment to tell you how our unlikely friendship started at St. Paul's Girls School in 1938. You know, I first met Anna in a place that seemed worlds away from the grim realities of war and resistance.

"She was a delicate soul, born into a middle-class Jewish family in Hanover, Germany, who were originally Polish Jews. She was just transitioning from being Ansel Grynzspan to Anna Adams as her family had recently fled the clutches of Hitler's persecution. They were now settling in a new home in Mayfair where her wealthy Uncle Benjamin lived. But Anna had just lost her little sisters to pneumonia, and her mother was very ill.

"I was the opposite of her in every way. The picture of youthful exuberance, always chasing after my next athletic pursuit, my sights set on the Olympics. But even amidst my own ambitions, I noticed Anna from the first day she came to our school. Tucked away in the shadows, lost in the pages of heavy literature books, while the other girls flitted about in their frivolity."

There was a warmth in Pearl's expression as she reminisced, her voice carrying a nostalgic undertone as she painted the scene.

"You see, I've always had a soft spot for the lost and the lonely, much like the stray kitten I once rescued from my grandmother's garden in

Normandy, or the injured duck I nursed back to health after it was struck by a car near Hyde Park. And Anna, with her quiet intensity and her thirst for knowledge, well, she captured my attention like no other.

"She may have been a misfit among the lipstick-obsessed and boy-crazy girls, but to me, she was a kindred spirit, yearning for connection in a world that often felt indifferent to her plight. I think Anna felt the same about me."

Pearl's light gaze wandered to Anna and the vulnerability shone again through her determined exterior.

"I sure did," Anna nodded. "Together with Henryk, you were a ray of sunshine in my life after a deep, dark night, Pearlie. And you always remained just that. A ray of sunshine."

"Thank you, *chérie, je'taime!*" Pearl blew Anna a kiss.

"When Anna secured her own place in Chelsea, she needed a flatmate, and who better to share it with than with her steadfast companion, *moi*? I was working down in Greenwich, elbows deep in grease and gears as a mechanic for the ATS, while Anna embarked on her own clandestine path to becoming London's spymaker."

Pearl's tone held a note of pride as she recounted their inter-twined lives.

"We weathered storms together, Anna and I, standing by each other's side as she extricated herself from a dreadful engagement to Count Roderick Macalister and found solace in the arms of the gallant, Polish, fighter pilot, Henryk 'Hubal' Pilecki, now her other half. He was the one who'd brought Anna's family to safety from the Polish borders in '38, a true hero in every sense. And like me, one of the few SOE agents who survived the concentration camps."

For a moment Pearl was silent, bowing her head in memory of the comrades they lost.

"When, in 1942, the opportunity arose for women to join the ranks of SOE agents, I begged Anna to let me be a part of it. The call of adventure was irresistible, and with my fluency in French, courtesy of my Maman, I was ready for whatever challenges lay ahead.

"Though Anna hesitated, reluctant to expose her dearest friend to the dangers that awaited, she relented in the end, knowing that my spirit was as indomitable as hers."

Once more, Pearl lowered her head, her voice carrying a softer tone as she spoke into the microphone.

"Perhaps I should have listened to my dearest friend. I still often feel regret for the anguish my disappearance caused my family and Anna. But then again, I couldn't have stood by idly while France, my second home, lay crushed under Nazi boots. *Pas moi*! Not I.

"And so, all's well that ends well. Anna found me and thanks to her, I came back home in body and spirit. I found love with another remarkable SOE survivor, Maurice Southgate. Anna and Henryk remain our closest companions. As for me, I've just begun to make a bit of a name for myself as a portrait photographer, while Anna, bless her heart, tirelessly works to finalize the files of the 102 agents from Section France who did not return.

"Let us raise a toast to all eight remarkable resistance women here on this stage, to the incredible survivors we've heard here speak. And, of course, always and everywhere, to the memory of those we've lost, and to the enduring legacy of those who fought for freedom. May their courage serve as a beacon of inspiration for us all.

"Lest We Forget."

With her closing words, Pearl's voice rang out with the fervent intensity that was her hallmark.

As the last echo of her words faded into the air, a wave of emotion swept through the audience. Applause erupted, echoing off the walls of Le Manoir, filling the room with a symphony of gratitude and admiration.

Standing ovations were given to each of the speakers and each of the Resistance Girls, honoring their bravery, resilience, and unyielding commitment to the cause of freedom.

Amidst the applause, the Alpine Harmony Quartet took up their instruments and the first long-drawn note of Nimrod from Edward Elgar's "Enigma Variations" mingled with the dying applause.

The piece carried a sense of solemnity, reverence, and unity, as a fitting and poignant honor to the bravery and sacrifice of those who'd fought for freedom during the second world war.

While the melodious notes weaved through the air like a comforting embrace, tears flowed, as much tears of loss and mourning as of unity and hope.

Then, the epicenter of it all, the conductor of this magnificent evening, Elsie Goldschmidt approached the microphone with a warm smile. Her voice carried across the room.

"I now announce the ballroom and the buffet to be open. Let us transition from words to dance and good food. Thank you, thank you, *merci beaucoup.*"

As the enchanting melody of The Blue Danube waltz filled the room, a wave of nostalgia swept through the audience. Memories of happier times intertwined with the bittersweet recollections of the struggles they had endured.

Couples rose from their seats, their hearts lighter despite the weight of the past. Hand in hand, they moved to the rhythm of the music, twirling and swaying in perfect harmony.

For those who had fought and survived, it was a moment of triumph, a celebration of resilience and camaraderie. Each step on the dance floor echoed the journey they had undertaken, from the darkest days of war to this jubilant gathering of souls united in courage and hope.

Amidst the joyous laughter and the strains of the waltz, there lingered an unspoken gratitude—a silent tribute to the sacrifices made and the lives lost in the name of freedom.

And as the evening unfolded, with laughter and tears mingling in the air, they embraced the promise of a brighter tomorrow, bound together by the enduring spirit of solidarity and love.

PART III

THE CHRISTMAS CARDS

DECEMBER 1948

27

ELSIE GOLDSCHMIDT

Six months later - Manoir de L'Espoir, Switzerland, 25 December 1948

The crackling of the birchwood in the fireplace filled Elsie Goldschmidt's office with a comforting warmth as she sat at her desk.

She was surrounded by the joyous flickering of candlelight, while the scent of pine from the freshly adorned Christmas tree prickled agreeably in her nose.

It was Christmas morning, and though not a Jewish celebration, Elsie was in a contemplative mood, stretching from over thirty years hiding in the Christian tradition to her early Jewish years in the Goldschmidt mansion in the heart of Vienna.

It had been a long haul and now she had come full circle. Outside her window, the frozen edges of Lake Geneva stretched out, its ice glistening under the pale winter sun.

A light dusting of snow blanketed the Swiss landscape, transforming the world into a winter wonderland.

Elsie's clear, blue eyes fixed on a man and a dog, venturing near the edge of the frozen lake, slipping and sliding, the crisp winter air tinged with the sound of the man's laughter.

The man was Abraham Blau, a retired history professor from Bonn University, a Holocaust survivor, and – knock her down with a feather – her very first beau during her first Opera Ball in 1916.

Abraham Blau, gray-haired, erudite and a widower who'd lost his wife and daughter in Ravensbrück while he survived Dachau, was now Elsie's significant other. And he was taking their beloved dog Fifi for a walk.

In that moment, surrounded by the scene of nature and the love of those dear to her, Elsie felt a profound sense of peace.

As her gaze lingered on the tranquil scene outside, her thoughts drifted back to the events of the past year.

For her, 1948 had been a year of profound change and new beginnings—a year marked by the closing of her finishing school Le Manoir and the opening of the Manoir de L'Espoir, a sanctuary for Holocaust survivors seeking solace and healing.

And then one day Abraham had walked in, and the unimaginable had happened. They had continued where they started thirty-two years ago, and it seemed like yesterday. Love was that simple when it was good.

She diverted her eyes from the lovely scene outside to turn to the stack of cards on her desk, cards she'd received from the Resistance Girls. She had saved them until now, looking forward to savoring their words in a moment of holiday bliss.

Memories of their shared struggles and triumphs flooded her mind. Their words of gratitude and affection during her June Anniversary – then only just returning to herself as Elsie Gold-schmidt - filled the former headmistress's heart with fondness.

How they had forged a new bond during those early summer days when the light was high, and their spirits soared.

In the quiet solitude of her office, remembering them so vividly, Elsie found herself overcome with a profound sense of gratitude.

Gratitude for the love and companionship of Abraham, whose gentle presence had brought light into her life.

Gratitude for the opportunity to make a difference in the lives of those who had suffered so much.

Gratitude for the simple joys of each day, cherished all the more in the wake of tragedy.

Gratitude for the transforming power of her Resistance Girls. Because, yes, she now thought of them as *her* girls.

She opened the first envelope with a delicate card of a Paris street in Christmas decorations. The message was simple yet heartfelt, written in Agnès's elegant handwriting.

Dear Elsie,

Merry Christmas to you and yours! I hope this card finds you in good health and spirits.

As 1948 draws to a close, I find myself reflecting on the profound impact our meeting in June has had on my life. Though I may not have had the privilege of attending Le Manoir like our dear friends, I now feel a special kinship with you and the extraordinary women you have nurtured and mentored.

Your wisdom and compassion know no bounds, and I am endlessly inspired by your resilience to start a new chapter in your life with Manoir de L'Espoir.

Alan, the boys and Océane still often talk of our

wonderful trip to Le Manoir and the absolute impeccable organization. To invite Capitaine Heurtier to pay tribute to me was so very kind of you!

As we embark on a new year filled with hope and possibility, I wish you all the health, happiness, and love you so deserve.

May your days be filled with laughter and light, and may your heart be forever warmed by the love of those who cherish you.

Please consider a visit to Paris in 1949. We would love to be your host.

With deepest gratitude and affection,

Agnès

THE NEXT CARD, enclosed in a mauve envelope scented with lily-of-the-valley, carried Madeleine's pointed handwriting.

Chère Elsie,

With great joy I extend my warmest wishes to you as the year draws to a close. It also gives me the opportunity to express my heartfelt appreciation for your kindness and understanding, especially in light of our past disharmony.

Of course, it remains my wrongdoing to disappear

without a trace from the school in 1918, but I'm glad you're now seeing it for what it was: youthful folly.

I am deeply thankful for the invaluable lessons you and your staff taught me during my time at Le Manoir, which have guided me in creating a loving home for my family at Lydden Valley.

Gerald, Lili, Isabella, and Sarah join me in fondly reminiscing about our reunion in June, and we are all delighted to see you thriving in your new endeavor at the Manoir de l'Espoir.

And Elle, of course, sends her special regards. It was so very thoughtful of you to invite my sister as my "tribute" to your own anniversary! Thank you for that!

Joyeux Noël et une très heureuse nouvelle année.

Avec mes sentiments d'amour et de reconnaissance.

Madeleine.

IN THE SAME mauve envelope was also Lili's card, showing a horseshoe decorated with holly leaves and tinsel.

My dearest Elsie,

I hope our cards fill you with the warmth of the holiday season.

At times I still feel myself basking in the wonderful anniversary celebration we shared last June. I hope this is the same for you! It was so thoughtful of you to invite Sarah, granting her the opportunity to share her remarkable story.

We are forever thankful for the chance to be part of such a profound experience.

Reflecting on our journey together, I must acknowledge my perception of you has evolved over time—from seeing you as "Madame Paul" to embracing the vibrant spirit of Elsie Goldschmidt.

I confess to misjudging you in the past, a realization that has served as a valuable lesson in refraining from forming hasty opinions about others. Your grace and your grit have left a profound impression on me.

In my weekly column for The Daily Worker, a British newspaper, I have taken inspiration from our shared experiences (without disclosing names) to caution against the dangers of making judgments based solely on appearances.

It is a lesson I am eager to share with my readers.

On a lighter note, Esther, Océane, and I - still the closest of friends- have planned a walking vacation in the Swiss Alps next summer!

Naturally, our itinerary includes a visit to the Manoir de l'Espoir, a place we are eager to explore and where we anticipate basking in the warmth of your hospitality once again.

Merry Christmas and a Happy New Year, also from Iain and Zack. We're expecting our next child in February, and I'll make sure to send you a birth announcement card.

Yours, Lili.

THE FOURTH CARD had a Paris stamp and was from Océane.

Dear Elsie,

I trust this card finds you surrounded by the joy of the holiday season.

May I express my deepest gratitude for your kind invitation to your anniversary celebration last June? It was a truly memorable occasion, and I am honored to have been a part of it.

I was particularly touched by your gesture in inviting Hans Arenberg, our "Good German", to join us on stage. It just shows your congeniality and generosity of spirit know no bounds.

As a result, the ties between Hans and Anna

Arenberg and our family have grown stronger, and they recently welcomed their son, Maris, into the world—a name they gave the little boy in honor of me, as it means "of the sea."

And on another note, if ever you find yourself with a medical question related to your guests at Manoir de L'Espoir, please do not hesitate to reach out to me.

As a cardiologist, I have encountered many heart ailments still connected to the war, and I am more than willing to offer my assistance and knowledge in any way I can.

Jean-Jacques, your co-conspirator in the June organization, sends you his warmest regards. Max and Bertrand are starting to walk and talk. Such delight!

Looking ahead, I eagerly anticipate the possibility of reuniting with you again next summer.

Wishing you a Merry Christmas and a joyous New Year,

With warmest regards,

Océane.

As Elsie took a break from reading the cards, the door creaked open, and Abraham stepped into the room. Abraham Blau was a towering presence, yet his demeanor exuded a gentle warmth that enveloped Elsie like a comforting embrace.

His tall stature was softened by a slight stoop, a testament to the years of excruciating manual work during his years in the camps.

His weathered hands, calloused from toil and torture, had a tenderness in the way he held the tray with two steaming cups of coffee and two slices of apfelstrudel, the sweet apple and cinnamon aroma wafting through the room.

Abraham's smile revealed gentle kindness and deep wisdom, the two characteristics most prominent in him.

The salt-and-pepper hair was neatly combed, and his dark eyes sparkled with affection as he addressed Elsie in his deep, reassuring voice, setting the tray down on her desk.

"Good morning, my dear. I hope I'm not interrupting?"

"Not at all, Abe. Just reading cards. I followed your daring venture at the edge of the frozen lake. Fie, you could have broken a leg or fallen in!"

"Not me!" Abraham chuckled. "*Hatsloche un broche,* we say in Yiddish, don't we? I'm sure the Brits stole that from us when they started using "break a leg" for good luck. Abraham pulled out a chair and seated himself across from her, his expression filled with affection.

"Where's Fifi?" Elsie asked.

"Oh, the little rascal is being warmed up in the kitchen and getting her biscuits. Maria promised to bring her in in a minute."

Elsie returned his smile, her heart as always fluttering with warmth at the sight of him. "Thank you for the coffee and strudel. It looks and smells delicious. Aren't we lucky with a cook like Maria?"

"We are, we are, my dear. Very lucky indeed." He reached across the desk to gently squeeze Elsie's hand. "I thought you might enjoy a little treat to start your day."

Her heart swelled with love for this man who had become her rock, her confidant, and her greatest source of strength. She reached for the cup of coffee, inhaling deeply the rich aroma, and took a sip, relishing in the uplifting warmth that spread through her body.

As they sat together in her once-stern, now-cozy office, surrounded by the memories of the past and the promise of the future, Elsie knew they both felt what needed no words.

A profound sense of gratitude for what life had bestowed on them, each other, their refuge home, the golden harvest years that came from long careers.

With Abraham by her side, Elsie was complete, at ease, just Elsie. There was no need for marriage or formal commitment. They had both lived and lost and found again.

The door creaked open once more, heralding the entrance of the reigning queen of Le Manoir de l'Espoir.

"Fifi!"

The lively, white Maltheser pranced into the room, her fluffy tail wagging with excitement. With a graceful somersault, she leaped onto Elsie's lap, her playful antics bringing a smile to her mistress's lips.

"Oh, you funny little thing! Can you not learn to behave?"

Fifi responded with a long stroke of her red tongue over Elsie's cheek, eliciting a chuckle from her mistress.

"That's enough, Fifi darling."

But Fifi had other plans. With a mischievous glint in her marble-like dark eyes, she darted towards the last crumbs on Elsie's plate, balancing on her hind legs as she reached for the tantalizing morsels.

Elsie sighed. "I think I was better at making young ladies behave than this little dog."

"Leave her to me, Elsa," Abraham laughed. With a gentle hand, he placed his plate on the floor, where Fifi eagerly pounced upon it.

Rising from his seat, he planted a kiss on Elsie's cheek, his affectionate gesture tempered by the lingering moisture of Fifi's tongue.

"Come on, Fifi, let the mistress read her cards in peace. I'll train you to become a well-behaved little damsel. See you at lunch, Elsa dear."

And with that, Abraham bid farewell, leaving the room with Fifi in tow and closing the door behind him with a soft click. How she loved the way he said "Elsa." It warmed her heart warm with great affection.

Returning her gaze to the cards spread out before her, Elsie reached for the next one with a smile, eager to immerse herself in the love and memories they held. This one was from her secret favorite, Esther.

Dearest Elsie and Abraham and all,

Tore and I wish you all a joyous holiday season filled with love and laughter. It warms my heart every time I think of the wonderful memories we shared during your visit to our Franz and Naomi Weiss Recuperation Center in September.

Seeing you both and being able to introduce our little Naomi to you, was another highlight of this wonderful year, 1948.

I'm delighted with the cooperation between our two institutes, and I look forward to many more fruitful collaborations in the future.

As for Tore, he remains as busy as ever with his full agenda as Minister of Social Affairs with the Norwegian Government.

However, he's been contemplating returning to his university studies in geology, which were unfortunately interrupted by the war. It would be a joy to see him pursue his passion once again.

Apart from looking after Naomi, I absolutely love working at the Recuperation Center. As it is the height of the skiing season, I spend as much time as I can giving my lessons. It amazes me every time how well traumatized people react to fresh air and healthy movement.

Naomi is a darling little thing and brings us all the joy in the world.

Looking ahead, Rebecca and Ben's wedding in March promises to be a joyous occasion, and I dearly hope that both you and Abraham will be able to attend.

Your presence would truly make the celebration complete.

Wishing you both a Happy Belated Hannukah and a Happy New Year filled with love, happiness, and good health.

With warmest regards,

Esther.

"OH, OH, OH!" Elsie heard herself mumble feeling herself tear up. How she loved that dear family and how she prayed with everything in her that Esther and Rebecca would find nothing but happiness going forward into the future.

If there was one family that deserved that it was the Weiss family.

Next up was her surprise friend, Sable. Oh, the past had been so complicated between them, but Sable had made immense growth during the war. And now she was none other than the British Ambassador for France.

Of course, Sable had always been a force to be reckoned with, but she'd turned that force to exceedingly good use after a rocky start.

My Dearest Elsie,

Warm greetings from Alnor Castle in Inveraray, where our family gathers to celebrate the joyous Christmas season.

I hope this card finds you and Abraham in good health and high spirits.

I must admit, being the ambassador to the UK in France has proven to be a demanding yet immensely fulfilling role.

The recent news of our expanding family has added an extra layer of excitement and anticipation to our celebrations.

Yes, you read correctly - in October we received the delightful news that I am expecting!

Isabella is positively ecstatic at the prospect of becoming a big sister, although she has already announced she will not refer to the child by its given name but will call it just "baby", so it knows its place until it comes of age. Much to Bill and my amusement, but probably not of the child in question.

Reflecting on our time together in June fills my heart with warmth and gratitude. It was a true joy to witness our bonds deepen and our friendships flourish. Please know that the memories of our reunion are cherished dearly.

As for Freddie and David, they are faring well. Currently, they are basking in the sunshine of the Bahamas, reveling in the beauty of the tropical paradise.

Meanwhile, Bill continues to excel in his pursuits, recently adding another poetry prize to his impressive collection.

With the baby's arrival expected in April, I anticipate being in London for the duration of the birth and the immediate aftermath.

However, rest assured that my intention is to return to Paris as soon as possible, eager to resume my duties and continue serving my beloved country.

Bill and I send you and Abraham our warmest wishes for a Merry Christmas and a joyous New Year.

May the holiday season bring you abundant bless-ings and everlasting joy.

Much love, etc,

Sable.

"ANOTHER BABY," Elsie mused, her heart swelling with joy. "Oh, how delightful! And for Sable, who suffered so much over the adoption of her first child, none of which I knew at the time when she was so difficult here at Le Manoir. It must be an extra bundle of joy to her."

She paused, reflecting on the journey Sable and Bill had traveled together. "And hadn't Bill lost a daughter as well? Oh, he must be in raptures, that big, rugged man with his poetic heart, who's broken open Sable's shell and made her shine. I'm positively so happy for them."

Two more cards remained: Edda's and Anna's. Both had been excellent students during their time at the Manoir, never causing any trouble.

Yet, even quiet waters could hold tremendous power. Both had demonstrated their fortitude during the war like no other. This is what Edda wrote:

Dearest Elsie,

As the holiday season approaches, I find myself reflecting on the profound impact of your work at the former finishing school.

Your dedication to create a resting place for Holo-caust survivors continues to leave me awestruck.

Each day, Ash and I are still reminded of the immense tragedies we and the rest of the Jewish community suffered during the war. The scars of that dark period run deep, and we are acutely aware of our loss and of those of so many families.

It is a somber reminder of the importance of preserving their memories and honoring their legacies.

On a lighter note, I am delighted to share the joyful news that Ash and I are expecting our next child, due to arrive in late January.

Our hearts are filled with anticipation as we eagerly await the arrival of our little one, who will be welcomed with open arms by our growing family.

Addey doesn't fully realize she'll be a big sister. She studies my growing belly with puzzlement, pointing to it and asking "baby?"

In other news, Ash and I are contemplating setting up a dance school together. Dance has always been our passion, and with me being unable to travel with two children, our own career is sort of on hold.

Ash doesn't want to hear anything about dancing with another partner, no matter that I urge him to continue performing.

Unfortunately, I must also share with you Jan has recently suffered a stroke. While it has been a challenging time for us all, I am relieved to report he is doing relatively well and sends his regards to you and Abraham.

Your support and encouragement have been a source of strength for us, and we are immensely grateful for your kindness.

Wishing you and Abraham a Merry Christmas (Asher sends Happy Belated Hannukah wishes!) and a joyous New Year filled with love, laughter, and cherished memories.

With love and gratitude,

Edda.

"I HAVE LOST count of the number of babies now," Elsie giggled aloud. "But it's all good. It's all good!"

THE LAST CARD, Anna. Serious, profound, Jewish, Anna. Elsie had known so little of her story during Anna's time at Le Manoir. Had she known the suffering that went on behind those dark-rimmed glasses, she would have been so much kinder to her. So much kinder!

Dearest Elsie,

As the year draws to a close, I find myself reminiscing about the wonderful anniversary celebration we shared in June.

Pearl and I often speak of the joyous moments we experienced together, surrounded by dear friends and cherished memories.

It was a truly unforgettable experience that has left a lasting impression on us both.

In light of our conversations, Pearl and I have been considering the idea of making another trip to visit you and your new center.

The work you are doing to provide a sanctuary for Holocaust survivors is truly commendable, and we would be honored to witness it firsthand.

Pearl, in particular, feels a deep connection to your cause, as she herself knows intimately what it is like to survive the camps.

She has expressed a desire to share her experiences with others, perhaps even through portrait photography if you and your guests would be open to such a path.

On a personal note, Henryk and Sarah are doing well, and I am pleased to report that our family is thriving.

We are eagerly awaiting the arrival of our second child in June, and the prospect of becoming parents once again fills us with joy and anticipation.

In addition, I am almost ready to conclude my investigations into the missing agents from SOE Section France. With only two more to trace, I am hopeful I will soon be able to bring closure to their families and loved ones.

As we look ahead to the new year, I am filled with gratitude for the wonderful friendship we shared in this one.

Your support and encouragement have been a source of great strength to us all and I'm absolutely certain not one of the Resistance Girls now regrets ever having been to Le Manoir under your tutelage.

We are immensely grateful for your wise lessons and our new-found friendship.

Henryk, Pearl, Maurice, and I wish you and Abraham a Happy Belated Hannukah and a Happy 1949.

And I personally wish you an ongoing wonderful friendship with your Resistance Girls!

With all my love and affection,

Anna.

As ELSIE SAT in her cozy office, surrounded by the soft glow of the fire and the lingering scent of coffee and apfelstrudel, she finally felt the apotheosis for the life she'd built.

All regret over her life's choices now melted, like the snow giving way to the heat of the sun on the tops of the Savoy Alps in spring.

The cards from her dear friends, her former students lay scattered before her, each one a new bond built on old ties. All they had shared and the journey they had chosen. How it all came together in this moment.

Closing her eyes, Elsie allowed herself to drift back in time, to the thirty years she'd spent as the headmistress of Le Manoir. Compassion for herself replaced the nagging feeling of guilt.

She remembered the countless young women who had passed through its halls, each one with their own hopes, dreams, and aspirations.

She'd watched them grow and flourish, guiding them with what she had, a tinge of wisdom and much strictness. With just one goal: to help them navigate the challenges of adolescence and emerge as confident, capable individuals.

But it was the Resistance Girls who held a special place in her heart. Their courage, resilience, their fight for freedom had inspired her in ways she could never have imagined.

They'd given her the final push to do what she needed to do. With all her heart, all her soul, all her love.

Totally embracing the Elsie Goldschmidt she'd always been, she opened the celestite eyes and glanced out the window. Her gaze fell on the frozen edges of Lake Geneva, the icy parts shimmering in the diffuse light of the morning sun.

The beauty of the scene before her served as a poignant reminder of the passage of time and the preciousness of each moment.

With a contented sigh, Elsie knew she'd made the right decision to close Le Manoir and start this new chapter of her life. Le Manoir de l'Espoir was more than just a center for Holocaust survivors—it was her beacon of hope, her contribution to the resilience of the human spirit, and her testament to the enduring legacy of the Resistance Girls.

And beside Elsie would always be her source of strength and support, Abraham. His steadfast loving presence was her lifeboat through the storm, his love her anchor.

As she reached for the cards once more, a smile tugged at the corners of her lips. Her smile held all the precious treasures, the friendships she now cherished and the journey she had undertaken.

With a heart full of gratitude, Elsie was exactly where she was meant to be, surrounded by love, warmth, and the promise of a peaceful tomorrow.

AFTERWORD

Writing the eight books of The Resistance Girl series has been an extraordinary journey for me, one that has lasted five years and has profoundly changed my life.

From the moment I decided I would center my books around the World Wars, it was also clear to me I should focus on the women. Women played pivotal, yet often neglected, roles during these tumultuous times in the first half of the 20th century. The idea that I should write about resistance women was a matter of connecting the dots.

During the early years of my writing career, I wasn't ready to write about the real women of the Resistance, as I felt I still had so much more research to do. So, I created fictive characters that acted against the real canvas of world war happenings.

Each Resistance Girl I created became a cherished character to me and I made it my mission to weave their stories into the fabric of history with all the care and reverence I could muster.

The two women from World War I, Agnès and Madeleine,

though they cannot be traditionally labeled as resistance fighters, embodied different aspects of the spirit of female resilience and bravery that defined the era. But they were ahead of their time.

Agnès, with her kind and gentle demeanor masking an unyielding will and unstoppable courage. For me, she symbolized the quiet strength of educated women who defy societal expectations to make their mark on history.

While historical evidence may not explicitly show female surgeons operating near the front lines during World War I, I felt it was crucial to elevate a 20th-century woman to a position of authority and agency in "In Picardy's Fields."

The fact is that there were female surgeons at the time, but they operated in hospitals in Paris and England, away from the battlegrounds. Through Agnès, I sought to highlight the resilience and resourcefulness of women when called to step up and do their bit where it was most urgent.

Personally, I have a deep respect for the medical professions, especially women following the call to heal in war situations, and I really wanted to deviate from the traditional role of the nurse and make her a surgeon.

MADELEINE, the fiery, redheaded rebel, who captured the hearts of many readers with her audacity and adventurous spirit and pet monkey LouLou, is a different woman all together. Still more, a daring teenager. In a time when women were expected to conform, certainly women of her class, Madeleine sought to challenge conventions, embodying the spirit of the pirate and frontier girls of lore.

She goes where the action takes her, even if that means donning the uniform of a deceased German soldier to enter her captured family château as a spy *avant la lettre*. Who doesn't like a fearless woman like that?

I read many adventure books when I was a kid and red-haired, fearless women like Boudica were certainly a model for Madeleine. Though my Boudica didn't command an army, she'd certainly have liked to!

LILI, Madeleine's daughter in "The Diamond Courier," embodies much of her mother's rebellious spirit. However, unlike Madeleine, Lili is driven by a desire to forge her own path and make a name for herself. Inspired by the "aristocratic rebels" of the 1930s who sought to challenge conservatism, Lili dreams of a career as a war reporter and a commitment to 'communist' ideals.

Her adventurous nature leads her to unexpected places, including the dangerous world of diamond smuggling, where she defies convention and risks everything for the thrill of the unknown.

Like her mother before her, Lili's journey is one of courage, defiance, and a relentless pursuit of freedom. As she navigates the treacherous waters of espionage and intrigue, she proves herself to be a true chip off the old block, unafraid to challenge the status quo and chart her own course through life's uncertainties.

Oh yes, I was quite the rebel in my younger years and love to splash those characters on the page. And a war correspondent? That's my other type of female heroism!

OCÉANE, Agnès's daughter in "The Parisian Spy," is a young medical student who embarks on a journey of self-discovery that defies the expectations of her family's medical legacy. Unlike her mother, who knew she wanted to be a doctor from a young age, Océane initially questions her path and yearns for the freedom of an artist's life.

However, Océane's inherent sense of duty and desire to help others eventually leads her back to the medical profession. But she embraces medicine on her own terms, finding fulfilment in the healing arts and the ability to make a difference in people's lives.

Despite her cautious nature, Océane shares her mother's fearlessness when it comes to standing up for what she believes in. Joining the Resistance in France, she harnesses her medical skills to aid the cause, demonstrating courage and resilience in the face of danger.

Throughout her journey, Océane undergoes significant growth, learning to tap into her innate bravery during active combat. Her precision as a physician proves invaluable, enhancing her effectiveness as a sharpshooter and earning her a reputation for excellence on the battlefield.

Despite her prowess in combat, Océane's true calling remains rooted in medicine, a profession for which – as I said - I hold the deepest respect. Also, returning to France – always to Paris where I was born many moons ago– is always a delight for me.

IN "THE NORWEGIAN ASSASSIN", Esther's character undergoes a profound transformation that delves into the depths of human resilience and the enduring power of the human spirit. Initially depicted as a sweet, loving, and caring individual with a promising high society future, Esther's world is shattered when she loses everything she holds dear – her entire family – to the atrocities of war.

Through her loss, Esther evolves into a vengeful warrior fueled by a relentless determination to bring to justice those responsible for her suffering. Yet, amidst her quest for vengeance, I was careful not to strip Esther entirely of her inherent kindness and warmth.

Instead, I sought to portray the complex psychological effects of trauma, depicting Esther as a character who grapples with the moral implications of her actions and wrestles with her conscience.

With Esther's journey, I aimed to convey the human cost of war and the toll it takes on individuals, both physically and emotionally. Despite her transformation into a formidable adversary of the Nazi regime, Esther's moral struggles serve as a poignant reminder of the enduring humanity that lies within us.

Writing Esther's character was a deeply introspective and soul-searching experience for me as a writer. Drawing from my own experiences of loss and adversity, I sought to imbue her story with authenticity and emotional depth, allowing her journey to serve as a beacon of hope amid the darkness of war.

In the end, Esther's resilience stands as a testament to the human capacity for survival and the enduring power of hope.

In "The Highland Raven," delving into Sable's character was another deep exploration of personal scars and the profound impact of loss. While I haven't experienced Sable's specific trauma of a forced adoption, I drew upon my own experience of losing a child, understanding the destabilizing journey that that leads to.

Sable presented a unique challenge as a character. I needed to ensure that readers empathized with her despite her flaws and occasionally reckless behavior. Her actions, often driven by trauma-induced desensitization, required careful portrayal to convey the complexity of her emotional state.

Despite the darkness of her past, Sable's journey is ultimately one of love and redemption. Her fierce and unconditional love for Freddie and Bill serves as a powerful force for healing, demonstrating that love has the capacity to overcome even the deepest wounds.

Yet, intertwined with her desire for love and connection is a sense of fearlessness, borne out of trauma and a desire to reclaim agency over her own life.

This duality is evident in her aspiration to become a secret agent, driven by both a longing for adventure and a willingness to confront danger head-on.

However, it is only through confronting the source of her pain, the biological father of her child, and realizing he is not the monster she'd imagined him to be, that Sable is able to undergo a profound transformation.

As she confronts her past and embraces her role as a resistance fighter, she finds strength and purpose in fighting for justice and freedom, ultimately finding redemption and a reason to live for.

EDDA IN "THE CRYSTAL BUTTERFLY" allowed me to fulfill a lifelong desire to delve into the enchanting world of ballet, a passion close to my heart.

While I didn't personally experience the struggles of Edda's Nazi-sympathizing parents, the theme resonates with my own family history. There's a shadow of collaboration with the Germans in my Dutch lineage, casting a stigma that lingered long after the war ended. I aimed to capture this legacy and the enduring repercussions it had on Dutch society.

Through Edda's character, I wanted to explore the profound dedication to a profession and the extraordinary lengths it can propel someone when fueled by discipline and passion. The lyrical nature of the book mirrors the elegance and grace of ballet, infusing the narrative with a sense of beauty and artistry.

Edda herself is not a complicated person, but her surroundings, torn between her Jewish boyfriend and Nazi-sympathizing parents, create a complex and challenging environment.

Her decision to join the Resistance is driven by necessity rather than emotion, reflecting her level-headedness and pragmatic approach to the cause. For Edda, it's simply what must be done, a call on her strength and determination.

FINALLY, ANNA IN "THE LONDON SPYMAKER" presents a unique portrayal of trauma and resilience. From the outset, Anna grapples with deep-seated trauma, exacerbated by the necessity to conceal her identity as a German-born Jew within the confines of the British Intelligence.

Unlike Esther or Sable, Anna's response to trauma is characterized by outward composure and detachment. She appears unaffected, even as tumultuous emotions churn beneath the surface.

Yet, beneath her calm exterior, Anna's emotions run profound and complex. She feels deeply, but her fear of vulnerability and rejection often leads her to suppress her emotions, burying them beneath layers of professionalism and perfectionism. A consummate workaholic, Anna strives tirelessly to prove her worth, pushing herself to the brink when she perceives failure.

In crafting Anna's character, I aimed to depict a woman deserving of boundless love and compassion. Despite the trials she endures, Anna's resilience and strength shine through, ultimately earning her the love and acceptance she richly deserves.

Her journey serves as a poignant reminder of the depth of human emotion and the power of love to heal even the deepest of wounds.

There's a lot of me in Anna as well! More than a lot!

·   ·   ·

As I bid farewell to The Resistance Girls , I feel so much gratitude for having been able to bring these remarkable women to life on the page.

May their stories continue to inspire and resonate with readers, reminding us that - no matter what the stakes are - love, courage and faith will always win.

Yours,

Hannah Byron

~

WHERE ONE STORY ENDS, **another begins!**

Dear reader, get ready for an exciting new journey with "Timeless Spies." On the next page, dive into a thrilling chapter about Lise de Baissac, the pioneering SOE agent parachuted into France in 1942. Experience the courage and intrigue of real resistance women.

Stay ahead of the game.

Join my newsletter and be the first to know about preorders and exclusive updates!

Newsletter link: https://www.hannahbyron.com/newsletter

THE COLOR OF COURAGE
THE JUMP

Mer-sur-Loire, 25 September 1942

It was a perfect night for a parachute jump. No clouds, no low-hanging mist, a full moon that rose into the sky like a giant snowball, casting an ethereal glow over the dense woodlands below. Just enough light for the pilot to maneuver the plane without headlights. The meandering Loire River glimmered beneath them like a glowing worm, the surface rippling gently in the reflection of the moonlight.

As Lise peered through the window of the Whitley bomber, her hopes soared. If tonight the reception team got their act together, Andrée Borrel and she would be able to jump. The weather wouldn't be the problem.

Yesterday had been such a disillusion. The pilot had refused to drop them because the flashlights at the landing site weren't as agreed. Only two lamps instead of three. Can you imagine? He'd turned the Whitley around and flew them straight back to RAF Tempsford.

All Lise could think was, "why?" But they'd had to sit through another arduous flight with the relentless drone of the engines vibrating through their bones.

Lise's behind was still sore from sitting on that hard aircraft floor all those hours with her parachute clinging to her back and the straps pressing into her skin.

But this was a new night and new chances, and she'd better laugh at herself for complaining about a minor discomfort like this. There'd be plenty of times she'd be a lot less comfortable on French soil, with Germans waiting to skin her alive if they could get their hands on her.

The cold night air seeped through the fuselage, carrying the scent of engine oil and the metallic tang of the aircraft. Andrée and she were the first "Janes" to be parachuted into France. So far the pilots had only escorted "Joes."

Yvonne Rudellat, who'd been with Andrée in the first batch of female recruits trained for SOE, had arrived before them, traveling by felucca via Gibraltar. If all went well this night, Yvonne would be waiting for them with the reception team down below.

They sat squashed in the small space with their legs drawn up, listening over the drone of the aircraft's engines for the sound of German anti-aircraft artillery. So far, so good.

To distract herself, Lise stared at the moon. It was as bright and lemony pale over France as it used to be during her childhood summers, watching it float up over the Trou aux Cerfs in Mauritius while sitting snugly between her brothers, Jean and Claude.

But no thinking of them right now. No thinking of the past, nor the future. She would only think of the moon, that benign beacon guiding their pilot to the right landing ground.

The night stretched before her like an endless expanse of ebony velvet, punctuated by the distant glimmer of millions of stars.

The roar of the plane's engine had reduced conversation with

Andrée to shouting short sentences in each other's ears. It became so exhausting they'd given up. Now Andrée was probably as huddled up in her own thoughts as she was herself.

The light of the moon followed the landscape below, illuminating the patchwork of fields and forests that blurred into indistinct shapes as they hurtled through the darkness.

Another flashback took her to the fields behind their house in Curepipe. Zigzagging through the tropical evening in a linen dress and sandals, occasionally blipping her flashlight to let her brothers know her position.

They'd left Mauritius twenty-three years ago. She'd lived in Paris, in London. Why did she find herself going back to her wild young years on the island in the Indian Ocean right now?

Because, after the long-drawn, boring years in the newsroom office, she was finally embarking on a real adventure again. The flashbacks reminded her of who she once was. Bold, confident, strong-minded.

Still, being a secret agent in occupied France would be far from child's play. Lise was very aware of the gravity of her situation, yet she found herself oddly detached, her emotions veiled beneath a veneer of icy composure.

She knew all the risks of this mission, not just because of Jepson's intense interview and her recent Beaulieu training, but also because she was that kind of person. She calculated and dissected every outcome of her actions like a skilled surgeon considers the steps of the surgery.

There was no room for sentimentality, for heroism, for fear. The world of espionage needed only cold, hard logic and a steely resolve to see the mission through to its conclusion.

As the Whitley Bomber of the Special Duties Squadron rumbled on, she glanced through the dusk at Andrée, who sat with her hands clasped around her knees, making herself as comfortable as possible by resting against her parachute.

Lise didn't know much about her as Andrée had been in the first SOE training for women and Lise in the second. Her companion looked tense, forlorn. She was very pretty with dark hair and regular features, at least fifteen years younger than Lise. She appeared to be a very charming, uncomplicated sort of girl.

Of course Andrée was tense. Why wouldn't she be? She was heading for the hub of Nazi-occupied France: Paris. Lise was bound for sleepy Poitiers. But Andrée looked like a tough cookie, and apparently, she was a hell of a wireless operator, much better at sending messages than she was.

Lise double-checked her equipment in the dark, fingers tracing the familiar contours of the parachute buckles, ensuring each strap was securely fastened. Her overalls felt constricting, a second skin clinging to her like a shield over her fashionable French dress, but not warm enough to protect her from the biting cold.

The Colt in the holster over her overalls felt like an out-of-place yet necessary accessory, but it was needed in case their reception team didn't have the tea ready. After her shooting drills she'd probably be capable of taking down a German or two even in a pitch-black forest.

Ugh, no thinking of that. She continued with her check, just to keep busy. The adrenaline kept her wide awake, though she usually wasn't a night owl. The folded switchblade sewn into her sleeve was another layer of security, though she hoped she wouldn't have to cut it loose from its rigging on arrival. The torch was in her leg pocket. All there.

Then her fingers touched a smooth flat case in another pocket. For a moment she hesitated. What was it? Oh, she'd forgotten. It was the golden cigarette case that Buck, nickname of the head of Section

F, had pressed into her hand at the airport. A gift to remind them of home. Well, she wasn't much of a smoker, but it was a kind gesture.

Tracing her finger over the embossed relief, she wondered what was imprinted there. She was too preoccupied when they finally took off, so she'd shoved the case in her pocket without a proper look. It was probably worth quite a bit.

At her side was her valise, strapped to its own parachute and containing the essential supplies for the widow Madame Irène Brisée, her alias. There was no room for error here, no margin for hesitation; every action must be executed with flawless precision if she was to evade capture by the Germans.

Apart from the agents and their luggage, there was also a crate with supplies for the French Resistance with its own parachute. Revolvers, ammunition, detonators, that sort of things.

The reception team would take care of the crate when it landed. Their job was to get out of these harnesses as quickly as they could and hide the parachutes.

"Orléans!" She pointed to Andrée, who nodded, staring unblinkingly out of her own window. The Whitley nosed down and headed towards Blois. The descent created a certain giddiness, but Lise breathed through it.

Let the flare paths be in place tonight. I can't stomach another return to England.

Her watch showed 0:50 a.m. Almost there. She peered and peered, but it was inky down below apart from the moon and the glistening river.

After only one parachute jump in the dark and on safe British soil, this was it. As the moment of truth drew near, Lise prepared herself to hurl her body into the abyss, in the knowledge that the fate of a free France was determined by the success or failure of missions like hers.

In the seconds that remained before the jump, she steeled her body and mind, knowing she must expect every possible outcome. This was the ultimate test of her courage and commitment, a matter of life and death. Once she plunged into the darkness below, she knew she must face her fate as expected from a trained agent.

"Remember I jump first," Andrée shouted in her ear. Lise gave her the thumbs up. She'd preferred to go first, as it was harder to follow and land near the first jumper, but they drew straws and Andrée had won.

The moments now stretched into an eternity. Lise felt a surge of adrenaline pulsing through her veins, heightening her senses to the highest degree. The deafening roar of the Whitley's engines faded into the background, replaced by the pounding of her heart, steady and rhythmic like a drumbeat in her ears.

She stole a last glance at Andrée, her features illuminated by the dim glow of the full moon, her eyes reflecting a mixture of trepidation and determination, mirroring Lise's own.

And then, without further warning, the moment arrived.

Dot. Dot. Dash. Dot: F

The correct Morse signals flashed up. Like the first tones of Beethoven's 5th.

Thank God!

"Jane 1 and Jane 2, ready yourselves." The crackling voice of the pilot sounded through his mouthpiece, and Lise felt the plane dipping even lower.

The dispatcher emerged from the cockpit and opened a hole in the bottom of the aircraft. An icy wind whistled through the open floor of the low-flying Whitley.

As the aircraft roared between the trees, she felt turbulent vibrations beneath her feet. Andrée sat on the edge of the hole, her feet dangling down. She gave Lise a final glance, her chin up defiantly. Then she was gone. Lise followed immediately, swift and soundless.

With a prayer on her lips and a resolve like tempered steel, she tumbled down, the rushing wind tearing at her senses as she plummeted toward the earth below.

Time seemed to blur, each passing second stretched thin like taut wire as the ground rushed up to meet her with terrifying speed. The sensation of weightlessness enveloped her, a fleeting moment of surreal tranquility amidst the chaos of the jump.

Her senses reeled as the world spun around her, the roar of the wind drowning out all other sound, leaving only the deafening thud of her heartbeat echoing in her ears.

With a sudden jolt the parachute snapped open above her, billowing outwards in a triumphant flourish of silk and cord. She gasped in awe as the world slowed to a standstill, the earth below stretching out before her like a vast canvas of shadows and light.

With practiced ease, she guided the parachute towards the ground where flashlights flickered at regular intervals, her hands steady as she navigated the swirling currents of air with precision born of earlier training. And then, with a soft thud, her boots made contact with the earth below. She'd done it.

In an equal puff of white cloth, she saw Andrée landed only a yard away. Thud, thud, thud. Their valises and the crate. As she scrambled to her feet, she saw three figures racing towards them. Their reception team, she hoped.

The Whitley took off over their heads, pointing its propeller upwards back to the bright moon. It was gone over the trees in seconds, leaving the moon for them. The only remembrance was the distant thrum of its engine. Back to England. Back to safety.

"*Je suis Pierre Culioli*," a French voice whispered in the dark, "welcome to the Resistance, mesdames. Let me escort you to your safe house."

Relief flooded through Lise's whole body on being greeted by friendly Frenchmen and not a German sentry. Fluid and still as night animals, the men buried their parachutes and collected their luggage. All was done within seconds. But there was no sight of Yvonne and no time for questions.

Lise's legs were wobbly, and her stomach churned, but her head was calm, happy almost. Well, now she was living on the soil of France! Who'd have thought that a few months ago?

As Andrée and she followed their guides, Lise felt a sense of accomplishment mixed with an appetite for what lay ahead.

COMING **24** SEPTEMBER.

Preorder here.

https://mybook.to/Revisited

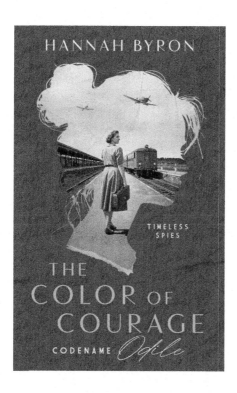

ABOUT THE AUTHOR

Hannah Byron was born to Anglo-Dutch parents in Paris, her heritage weaving together a varied tapestry of European cultures.

Currently based in Holland, she writes gripping Historical Fiction series centered around WW2 Resistance Women.

A former academic, Hannah's transition to full-time writing is a dream come true – or perhaps a sneaky plot hatched by Uncle Tom Naylor, whose heroic D-Day exploits sparked her obsession with WW2 history.

In her bestselling "The Resistance Girl Series", Hannah's heroines traverse Europe much like their adventurous creator. From the bustling streets of Paris to the polder-land countryside of Holland, to the cold maintains of Norway, her stories paint a vivid portrait of wartime heroism and resilience.

Her upcoming series, "Timeless Spies", focuses on female secret agents and their daring exploits in France and Britain during WW2.

With a nod to her lineage and a wink at fate, Hannah's novels celebrate strong women, blending romance with resilience.

Each page pays homage to the unsung heroines of the 20th century, who got dirty in overalls, flew planes, and did intelligence work in the name of liberty and love. These early adopters serve as a poignant reminder of the legacy left by the trailblazing women who paved the way for future generations.

But that's not all! Under the pen name *Hannah Ivory,* she writes Historical Mysteries, whisking readers away on Victorian adventures with the intrepid Mrs. Imogene Lynch.

ALSO BY HANNAH BYRON

The Resistance Girl Series

In Picardy's Fields

The Diamond Courier

The Parisian Spy

The Norwegian Assassin

The Highland Raven

The Crystal Butterfly

The London Spymaker

The Resistance Girls Revisited

Timeless Spies Series

The Color of Courage (Preorder)

The Echo of Valor (Preorder)

Spin-off novellas Resistance Girl Series

Miss Agnes

Doctor Agnes

AS HANNAH IVORY

HISTORICAL MYSTERIES

The Mrs Imogene Lynch Series

The Unsolved Case of the Secret Christmas Baby

The Peculiar Vanishing Act of Mr Ralph Herriot

Printed in Great Britain
by Amazon

57792090R00148